By the same author
SHEN OF THE SEA
E. P. Dutton & Company

Fan Shih hastened to tell her father what had happened.

THE WIND THAT WOULDN'T BLOW

Stories of the merry Middle Kingdom for Children, and myself

BY

ARTHUR BOWIE CHRISMAN

AUTHOR OF "SHEN OF THE SEA"

WITH SILHOUETTE DECORATIONS CUT BY

ELSE HASSELRIIS

NEW YORK
E. P. DUTTON & CO., INC.

Copyright, 1927

By E. P. DUTTON & COMPANY

All rights reserved

First printing	. . . July, 1927
Second printing	. . Sept., 1927
Third Printing	. Sept., 1928
Fourth Printing	. . Sept., 1928
Fifth Printing	. . . May, 1940

Printed in the United States of America

FROM END TO END
FROM FRONT TO BACK
THIS BOOK
FROM AN TO YAN
IS DEDICATED
TO
E. B. GARNETT

Kansas City Star please copy

FOREWORD

LIKE the outlandish old beggar, Sun Swee, who apologized first, and then smote His Majesty, Hu Sung, most grievously upon the side-face, I apologize for these so terrible stories before ever the reader has experienced his hurt. And hand in glove with the beg your pardon must go an explanation. Some of the tales here presented were old in China long before King Chieh Chung discovered the marks by which one might write. They were tongue-tales, passed from story-man to story-man, in the bazaars and over the camp fires. Others are no older than yesterday; the time when I first learned to hold a pen. All of them have been carefully changed to agree with the facts as they were, or really should have been and I wish them to be considered merely as stories—not as a teaching. Another point to make clear, or drive home, or whatever one is supposed to do with a point. . . . This book is no attempt at belittlement of the Chinese people. Emphatically not. My liking for the Chinese is high. Whenever there's a chance I speak good words of the country and the people. True enough, I bring to light some few small unusualities, but they are to be found in every peopled portion of the world. And for every wicked king in mention, I have sought to introduce a praise-deserving farmer.

*   *   *   *   *

What follows is in sadness. The Philadelphia North American, so old and kindly —once on a time the paper of Benjamin Franklin—bought two or three of these stories. It gave me permission to use them in the book. Alas—never again will my stories have print in the paper of Franklin. For the North American has gone to the Land of the Long Dark Shadows. The presses have stopped forever. And I who tried so hard to tell the merry tales, now mourn for a friend departed.

                                        A. B. C.

CONTENTS

ILLUSTRATIONS

THE WIND THAT
WOULDN'T BLOW

THE WIND
THAT WOULDN'T BLOW

THE SHEN OF COLORED CORDS

AH CHOY was the one who gathered herbs, and his father, Doctor Chen Twom, pounded them and brayed them and mixed them in elixirs. The best and most money-bringing herbs grew around and about a set of hills

known as The Dragon's Lost Teeth. Those
were the wild and forbidding hills. Cannon-
like rumblings came up from reverberant cav-
erns, and fearsome shrieks could be heard.
Chinless ghosts walked there in the day's
bright light. But, except for Ah Choy, the
village folk walked there never.

It is pleasant work to gather simples,
and murmur "One, Two, Three," in counting the money thus gained. Contrariwise, it
is most embarrassing to know that a ghostly
hand is clutching for one's flying coat. The
people of Always In Shadow Village often
told Ah Choy beware. "You will have grief
in the hills. Mark our words, Ah Choy.
You'll lose your queue. And we are being
very kind, not to make your loss far greater."
But the boy merely laughed, and would not
be advised. Mmmmmmmm.

On a fair day in the after part of a summer, Ah Choy sat down in the hills to rest.
His basket was over-filled with herbs. He
thought he might laze in the shade of a
laurel, and perchance take a bit of a nap.
Just as his eyes were closing, a sound like

double thunder made him start. The earth trembled so violently that Ah Choy was shaken like a bean on a beaten drum head. He grasped a laurel and roved with his eyes to perceive the source of disruption.

Close by was a towering granite cliff. Ah Choy's eyes beheld a door in the rock swing open. Out stepped a man with a burden on his back—a hundred weight in a hempen sack. He was an oldish person, of malignant, leering face. His sack was well tied. Nevertheless, it was plain that he carried money. Coins disclosed their shapes against the cloth, and their redness gleamed through the mesh. Furthermore, as the old man walked, he made a clinking sound. He hastened past the cliff and disappeared.

Ah Choy crawled from under his sheltering bush and crept to the cliff to examine. He could find no mark of a door. There was not even a foot print to show whence the man had come. Ah Choy now grew uneasy in his mind. He began to realize that he had seen magic. He knew that in wisdom he should go instantly away from the place.

Yet his curiosity whispered coaxingly, "The old man has gone. Why be afraid? Of what use are our eyes if not to see, and learn new things?" Aloud, Ah Choy promised himself, "I shall toss a copper cash in the air. If the King's mark falls uppermost, I shall go home. If the other side—I shall stay and explore—until a ghost, or worse, a demon, desires my queue." He felt in his girdle purse for the single coin therein. His copper went up, and stopped, and turned. Came it down, and rolled against the cliff.

Again the hills echoed with that appalling roar. A wind came out to spin Ah Choy, and wrestle him to earth. When finally he opened his eyes he found himself almost within a spacious stone doorway. And he ventured. Taking two steps, and stopping, then taking two more, he slowly entered the cavern. A scribe's desk stood near to the portal. It held an enormous book. Ah Choy could read— such easy characters as *yin*, and *shan*. He glanced at an open page. "Wen Chiang. Always In Shadow Village. 5,137." So much the explorer read, but he could see no sense to it. Farther back he ventured, first with misgivings, then with as much joy as astonishment. Stacked in neat piles, red tier upon gleaming tier, he saw gold. Here was

Clink, clink, clink,—into the bag went fortunes.

a stack of golden bars, far higher than his head. Here was a bin of molded coins. Nearby were pearls, filling many rooms, each larger than a king's throne chamber. Scattered upon the pearls were bones, and from them came unsteadily, a baleful, bluish light.

Ah Choy wandered on. He beheld sparkling gems he imagined must be diamonds. He knew the rubies when he found them, for he had once seen a ruby button on a high mandarin's hat. He wandered on and wandered on. A softness underfoot caused him to stoop. Instead of a priceless carpet, he found a hempen sack. So much the better, he thought. The boy climbed into a bin of gold and used his hand in pleasant labor. Clink. Clink. Clink. Into the bag went fortunes. Again Ah Choy heard the terrible roar, but this time it caused him no trembling. It never occurred to him that the noise might be caused by a closing door. He was thinking only of gold, the wealth upon his fingers.

Ah Choy staggered and moved slowly. His need was for a giant's strength to bear away the treasure burden. At last he came to the door. It was closed. Not an inch of separation showed at the latch side. And still the adventurer felt no uneasiness. He saw a thousand bones upon the floor—and still he experienced no rise of fear.

The bearer of wealth placed his back to the

door and pushed. He might as well have tried to push Mount Tai away from its hard foundation. Then he remembered that he was face to face with magic. He set his sack upon the floor and pushed harder. The door opened a hand-width. Much heartened, he braced his feet, and thrust with all the power he had. His toes slipped, and down he went, sprawling. His sleeve pouches had been filled with gold. Now they were quite empty. Round pieces of gold, each in size a year's good living, wheeled helter-skelter across the cave. The boy had only one coin remaining —a little piece which had slipped into his shoe.

Ah Choy stepped back a dozen paces from the door. He rushed forward, and when he struck the granite barrier his force was that of a tiger to the kill. The heavy hinges shrieked. Out . . . into the sunlight reeled Ah Choy. . . . Safe???

Not so. . . . The cavern door passed shut upon his shoe. One of his heels was caught between stone and stone. The pain was very great. For a moment his eye saw only black-

ness. But the fainting weakness left him,
and he took out his knife and reached downward. From the cut in his shoe fell a small
golden coin. Backward it rolled, under the
door. Immediately the boy's foot came free.
But a twitch at his head caused renewed
pain. His braided hair had been snipped by
the door. His queue had been sheared in
two.

Ah Choy limped home and told his story.
For proof he exhibited the cut in his shoe.
And there was his queue, so sharply shorn.
The village laughed from end to end. "We
told him beware. Ho. Ho. Ho. He lost
his queue. Next time his loss will be greater.
Perhaps his head, perhaps his heart." Ah
Choy's father said, "Stay away from the hills,
my son, and settle into a less venturesome
business. Look at the mandarin, Wen
Chiang. Only today, while you were risking
your life in the hills, the mandarin sat safe
in his yamen and had a profit of more than
five thousand gold."

But Ah Choy was young and he loved the
hills. Next day he was back again, and the

simples were easier to find. Under an outward leaning cliff he paused, alarmed. No other person could be seen in the narrow valley. Hence he was much surprised to have heard a loud sneeze, where no sneeze was supposed to be. He glanced across the way and beheld an old man, seated in a cave; in the cavern's front, where sun-gleam fell upon him. The man had a pleasant face. There was no wickedness in his eyes, and none to his mouth.

Ah Choy wished some courage into his legs and shortly crossed to the cavern. He said, "I hope your chop sticks did good duty. I hope you had rice and pork lumps for all of a pleasant hour." The grey-beard answered, "Thank you, yes. . . . Kerchoo." He started quite an echo with his sneeze. The whole valley seemed to have a cold. Ah Choy decided he could be of service. "Honorable Mr. Cavern-man, in my pouch I have an excellent sneeze cure. My father is a doctor, Chen Twom his name, and he made me carry this medicine, for I too have a sneeze." The man accepted Ah Choy's remedy, and thanked him, adding, "It is cold and damp in my cave, so I came out here to sit in the sun and get well. I dislike to sneeze, for only now I nearly broke a thread." He had in his lap a sheaf of red cords, and at his side a sheaf of blue. "The cave is entirely too dank. I'm glad to say it isn't my usual dwelling place. That's on the moon, but when the moon is in the black I come down here and continue my work." He selected a blue thread and a red thread and tied the two together. It was curious business. Ah Choy wished to see more of it. He decided to keep up the talk, and so have an excuse for staying. "Do you know the gentleman of the other cave, the cave that has such a din-making door?" The matcher of threads answered, "I know him well—a brother of mine. He is the Shen who sees to it that people receive the wealth due unto them. He has all names in a book. If you, for instance, are ever to have a thousand ounces of silver, your name is in his book." Ah Choy exclaimed regretfully, "Then I wish I had gazed longer upon the ink." The old man glanced questioningly over his spectacles. "You surely don't mean that you were in my brother's cavern? But of course you were not. You could never have opened the door to leave." Ah Choy said, "I came to the door empty-handed, and it swung and let me depart. But I'm still crippled in the heel. Is my name really in the Money Shen's book?" The ancient one chuckled. "If your heel is lame, then it's clear you had a coin in your shoe. A good thing you dropped it. The bones in the cave were at one time men, who held to what they had. But you are a fortune's favorite. Yes, your name is in the book, for satisfying wealth—when you are older. I don't remember the year, but you will receive money quite early. Don't be like so many others. Many men are listed to receive their wealth very late, and so, as the poverished years are numbered past, they lose faith, and hope goes from them, and they drink *sam shu* and die tipsily, without waiting for their due. This is good sneeze medicine. I hope you will not lose hope."

Ah Choy replied, "Thank you. I shall keep it all. Does it matter if I ask you what interesting work you are doing?" He of the cavern frowned, but it seemed to be caused more by his task than by Ah Choy's question. At all events, in his own good time, he answered good-humoredly enough. "These blue silken threads represent maids—in the village —in the kingdom—in the world. The red threads represent men. I tie a certain blue thread to a given red thread—and that girl, some day, is to marry that man. I am The Shen Of Colored Cords, The Shen Of Marriage Destiny. Just now I tied two cords that make me sorrow. The girl is beautiful and good—and knows how melon seeds should be toasted. The man is a scamp. I wish I had found a better red thread, a better husband for the maiden."

Again Ah Choy dared. "Have you—have you a string to represent me? If so, good Grandfather Shen, will you not tie the thread of me to the blue thread you admire so greatly? I'd like to be sure of just such a wife, in the days when I take on the stature of a man." The old man opened his mouth to laugh. Only two teeth were in it. He

These blue silken threads represent maids.

had worn off the others, nibbling thread. "Heh, Heh, Heh," he chuckled. "I matched your thread a year ago, one day when I saw you here in the hills. The names have been written in fadeless ink. Too late. Too late to change. But, I'll tell you this. . . . I did most exceeding well by you. If I were younger, I'd play you a trick—Ho! Ho!— and take the maid for my own."

Ah Choy was crow-hopping up and down in his excitement. "What blue cord, good Grandfather Shen? Who is the maid I'm to marry?" The Shen matched several threads before he would speak. Once he frowned, and twice he smiled. "It is seldom indeed I disclose my secrets. But you look like a sensible boy. The girl is Fah Chih (which means Little One; an often heard nickname). And you . . . are fortunate."

Ah Choy stared out at the opposite cliff. And it was a highly uninteresting cliff— nothing but thunder-blackened granite. The boy stared and continued to stare. Finally he said, "I thank you, Grandfather Shen, for telling me these things. Now I must go home. I hope you lose your sneeze quite soon." The grey-beard said, "Walk slowly." That is the usual speech of parting.

When Ah Choy, with herbs, reached home he told his father of all sights and words, exactly as he had seen and heard in the cave. And he complained, "Honorable Father, I do not like this marriage-to-be. Fah Chih is a very good girl, and her father is an upright man. But, her father is only a woodcutter. I will be a wealthy man, and no doubt I could marry a palace born princess. Fah Chih I don't want." His father said, "I understand your feelings, perfectly, and I don't blame you in the least. But have patience. Perhaps in time it will grow upon you to like this woodcutter's child. Remember, it is a risking tongue that says 'No' to a Shen." But Ah Choy declared, "Shen or no Shen. Risky or not. My wife won't be Fah Chih."

Often when Ah Choy went to the village well he saw the woodcutter's daughter. Not very mannerly perhaps, but to save him he couldn't help staring. "So this freckled, ugly little girl is the one I'm to wive. Mmmmmm. I'll show the Shen a trick. I'll cut his colored cord apart, and use each end to tie up herbs for drying." Fah Chih had dimples in her cheeks. Those dimples haunted Ah Choy. He thought nothing could be uglier. He disliked the way Fah Chih held her head. He thought her voice too metallic. Her other faults were worse—and many. "My wife indeed. The Shen is a meddler. I'll never marry Fah Chih. I won't, and so, I won't. I'll go upon a travel. A thousand li the road is long to Chang An, the King's fair city, but I'll walk every step, if I must, and stay forever, if I need, to avoid this marriage that vexes me."

And the thought of travel stayed with him, but changed in its stay, and became an urge of ambition. He had often wished that some day he might sit in the Hall of Examination, might graduate and become famous. He said to his father, "Honorable Doctor Father, I wish to go away and become a scholar. I shall be a ta jin. My childhood is past. You have been kind to me, but I am growing, and I must go." His father replied, "I knew this would happen, my son, and so, I have prepared. Arrangements are made. In a week you may go to Chang An City. The scholar teacher Hoy Fung lives in that place. Obey his every order, and become a learned man."

Ah Choy was glad. The Shen's colored cord must surely break, when stretched the road of a thousand li. Ah Choy was sad. Chang An City stood far from home, under a different sky. And the life would be new, and the people strange, and no kind father to laugh away the sadnesses.

Time is sure in its passing. Slowly, perhaps, but faithfully, the wanted days at last appear. The morning of Ah Choy's departure lighted all the hills. The boy and his father ate their last breakfast together. Doctor Chen spoke of other sorrows, to keep away the thought of one his own. "Much sickness is in the village. I shall be very busy. Hu Chay, the coppersmith, is under his quilt with forty ills for company. Mostly imagination. The last herbs you gathered should soon stand him up in his sandals, ready for work again. About Mee Shao's little girl, I feel despair. She ran beneath a falling tree. Her head. It is very bad. I have told Mee Shao I see no hope." Ah Choy said, "Mee Shao's little girl? Do you mean the child Fah Chih?" Doctor Chen answered, "Yes. Fah Chih. Hadn't you heard of the disaster? Poor Chu Pi has had another seizure. Old Mrs. Woo has fits again." So the doctor rambled on, discussing this case and that. After a long silence Ah Choy murmured, "I am sorry the child Fah Chih . . . must go . . . to The Land of The Long Dark Shadows." And all the while a caravan was making up in the market place.

Bells were tinkling from the trappings of the red varnished saddles. Men were shouting, go and come. Camels snarled and bubbled, and the little donkeys sighed. Bales were corded tightly. Vaunting spearmen jangled to the fore. And thus the caravan set off on its thousand li, through the mountain passes and the desert plains, through heat and cold, through storms and bandit harryings, on the ancient way to Chang An City.

Once more the dust settled down in the pass road. The village took to its work of the day. Doctor Chen sadly went his rounds, with medicines and fireworks, to outwit the demons of sickness. "Poor old Mee Shao. I must do what I can. Must do what I can to save his little girl. But alas, I see no hope. If that coppersmith doesn't get out of bed I'll give him the worst tasting medicine I know."

Chang An, the beautiful, the city of desires fulfilled. . . . Ah Choy had capable teaching. In Chang An City why shouldn't he? Early and late it was study. He opened his books in the morning before he opened his eyes. All through the day, by sun he studied, into the night by candleshine, and when his candle flickered out he read in the glow of the moon. Young. Young. He was still a boy when his teachers said, "We can do no more. And we are proud."

So, Ah Choy, under his newly taken Flowery Name, "The One Who Heals With

Herbs," and a little mustache to give him dignity, began his practice. A doctor, he, like his father before him. In the town where

Early and late it was study.

Ah Choy—that is to say The One Who Heals With Herbs—chose to practice, dwelt a mandarin named Sheng. This gentleman took to his bed with an illness too hard to spell.

Doctor Ah Choy came to cure him. The good old medicines, vervain and gin seng, struck hard at the sickness-demons. The patient's stout will had a share in the recovery. His niece was a third, and very valuable, aid. The niece was named Mee Kuay—Rose. Most people thought her a remarkably bright young woman. Doctor Heals With Herbs perhaps did not. Or, perhaps he thought the young lady forgetful. A dozen times each visit he'd instruct her, "Now do not let your uncle arise. And . . . er . . . give him his medicines at the proper hours. And . . . . And. . . ." And then he'd talk of other things.

Good attention and terrible medicine soon made a well man of the mandarin Sheng. He said to his learned physician, "I hardly think you need come to see me tomorrow. I am perfectly fit. Couldn't possibly get any better."

But . . . who was it came the next morning so early? Ah Choy. Ah Choy came. And this Ah Choy young man, this brilliant doctor, was in a deplorable condition. He was

extremely nervous. It was difficult for him
to speak. He cleared his throat to say
"Pleasant." And cleared it again to say
"Rice." And that's "Good morning." But
he had come for more than Pleasant Rice.
"I . . I . . er . . . that is. Mmmmmm. I
have been talking to your adorable niece."
The mandarin said, "Have you?" Though
he must certainly have noticed it. "Oh, yes,"
Ah Choy assured him. "You must pardon
me, Honorable Mandarin, for not sending a
go-between (arranger of marriages), to discuss the matter, but I feared the go-between
might blunder. Honorable Mandarin, will
you please let me . . . er . . . marry your
niece? I . . . we . . . she. . . ." The mandarin answered, "Like you, I hardly know
what to say. My niece comes from a distant
part of the kingdom. Perhaps she would
not care to live here always. Perhaps her
father has already selected a husband for the
child. But. . . . Oh, well. I'll see. I'll see."

Day after day Ah Choy returned. At last
Mr. Sheng took pity on him and said, "Oh,

well. Go buy a saddle." And a saddle is used in the marriage ceremony.

Young Doctor Ah Choy sat beneath the moon window with Mee Kuay. He said, as young men will, "You are very unlike other

This golden shield covers a great misfortune. When I was very young and small, I was struck by a falling tree.

maidens. Your words are different, and your eyes—even your hair." Mee Kuay replied, "I pin my hair in this manner for a secret reason. And I must tell you why." She removed the gem-set combs and the ivory bodkins, and swept the long hair back over her shoulders. High upon her forehead gleamed a tiny golden plate. "This golden shield covers a great misfortune. When I was very young and small I was struck by a falling tree." Doctor Ah Choy's face became pale, and he said, "My own dear love, did you, perchance, once live in the western regions?" Mee Kuay answered, "Yes. My home was the village called Always In Shadow, a thousand li to the west."

THE SONLESS KING

KING CHWAN held speech with his chancellor. "Faithful Wang, today I am ninety-one oi two. I am old, old,—but the years have done me little harm. My thoughts are clear. My knees are supple. Arrange me some music, for I am happy. The world is at peace, and the paulownias are fragrant. Where is my fan, Wang? Send in a poet to tell me why my paulownia blossoms are purple."

The chancellor said, "Your Majesty, we, all of us, your people, rejoice that you have reached happy old age. Ninety-five years today. We are glad. So glad." (But his face was unsmiling.) "You have ruled justly, and the land is fat with rice." (He fumbled in his silken sleeve.) "Spiders rear their sons in our drums of war." Urged by nervousness, he gestured, and a paper dropped to the floor. "What's that?" asked the King. "A well-wishing letter from one of my mandarins?" The chancellor trembled. "It is only a very weak poem I've composed. Not worth reading. O King, Paramount and Invincible, again hear my congratulations." He backed away from the throne, trying to smile, but nearer by far to weeping.

"You are the one with a dragon's heart," said chancellor to master-of-treasure. "You are the one to tell our King of this sorrow . . . and see him die. His heart is so sadly enfeebled that the slightest blow will kill him. But . . . it's your duty to show him the Western Tiger's writing." "Not mine," declared the treasurer. "It's fond I am of the

grey old King, and *I'll* never cause him an-
guish. A headsman's work is killing. Let the
headsman tell him of this evil." A hopeless
sigh. "The headsman's strength has gone
away. He moans in the farther garden."
"Then read the letter, again, aloud, and let
us combine our minds in thought."

So the chancellor opened a letter:

Read this. Respect this writing. Tremble
seven times, and obey. I, Sheng Hu, Ruler
of the Westward Country, demand tribute.
Ten thousand catties of gold I must have.
My soldiers are large and numerous. In
sleep they cry, "War—Give us war." Ah,
they are fierce. Finest gold of the mine I
must have—Ten thousand catties.

"We have half that many catties in our
vault," mused the treasurer. "Send it," said
Chancellor Wang. "But don't quite empty
the coffers. Remember, the cook's salary is
unpaid. Send what we can spare, and perhaps the threatening western king will be
satisfied. It's our only hope, for the army

is utterly untrained. The soldiers haven't fought for eighty years." "Softly," said the treasurer. "Has my life no value? The King would be furious if I sent gold without a royal order." The chancellor sank to the floor. "Completely true. And His Majesty might begin to suspect, if we asked him to sign the order. Oh, my head—why won't it think, and save the realm?" "I can think," declared the treasurer. He whispered to his quaking friend. The careworn face took on a smile. "Capital."

With a great joy giving him dancing steps, the chancellor went to the throne room. Said he, "I know you will say, 'Shen hao, Chancellor. Jolly well done,' when I tell you we have captured the Wolf Mannered bandit, with all his wealth, and have him secure." The King said, "Shen hao, Chancellor. Jolly well done. Now our last trouble is ended." The chancellor laughed. "Soon. Soon. Your Majesty. There is only the small matter of putting your seal upon the paper of execution—the death warrant." "Quite true," remarked His Majesty. "Where

are my spectacles with square gold frames?
No. Where are my lacquered frame spectacles? They have mee tsing (tea-stone)
eye pieces, and give better views. Also, they
look better."

⌣ Most cleverly, the chancellor tucked all
spectacles within his sleeve. It was for the
King's own good, he thought. "Do not weary
your eyes with looking, Majesty. I shall
place a finger on the paper, and there you
set the seal. Let my finger guide you." So
the King's tremulous hand bore down on the
seal, and the paper was legal and proper.

Meanwhile the treasurer, far underground,
was weighing his gold and counting. Heavy
steps descended the stair. The master-of-
treasure put string on a sack. "Is it Wang?"

"It is Wang."

"Is it well?"

"It is well."

"Is it written?"

"It is written."

"Then, here is the gold. Send it on to the
west."

Days of a month or more went past. The

chancellor fidgeted with a fan. The master-of-treasure wrote, over, and over, and over, "Lost. Lost. Lost." The comptroller of the four eminences sobbed. "Read it again," demanded the chancellor. The treasurer croaked, raven-like.

"Read this. Read twice, and thrice. Tremble seven times seven. You sent to me, to ME, *the King of the Western Country, three thousand catties of gold. Much of it is weakened with copper. Is that not shameless? My soldiers are thumping their drums. Their feet are treading to the battle march. My soldiers will bring me the gold I desire. And my soldiers will bring me a* MONARCH'S HEAD. *This is war."*

Now the comptroller of the four eminences was writing, "Lost. Lost. Lost. Lost." He was too sad to speak. The treasurer bowed his head. A page pranced up and announced that the King would speak to the chancellor.

The sovereign put tragedy into his words.

"Chancellor, I am giving up my kingship. I, who should be so happy, am sad. My people avoid me. I see them whispering in corners. They do not like my rule. Gaze into the mirror, Chancellor. Observe the irk upon your brow. *You* are dissatisfied, and the treasurer, and the cook—all have been moody this whole month gone. You like not your King . . . and, your King resigns. There is no blood of mine to reign. I am sonless. But you, Wang, are just, and you know the affairs of state. *You* shall rule upon the throne I leave."

The chancellor thought of a letter in his sleeve. He shuddered as he thought of it. In the last line of that letter was this, "And they will bring me a monarch's head."

"Please, Your Gracious Majesty," whined the chancellor, "I am no fit person to be King. I . . . I have a mania for drinking *sam shu*, and for roistering. I'd soon beggar the realm. For a King, take the master-of . . . (He remembered only in time that the master-of-treasure was his friend) Take. . . . Take someone other than me."

"Until this day I never knew you drank *sam shu*," said His Majesty. "It is hard to believe. But, you were about to mention the master-of-treasure. Send him in."

The treasurer shook till his ear-rings tinkled. "Oh, no, Your Majesty, I couldn't, couldn't be King. I . . . I suffer with red rages. I could never be fair-handed and kind. Let me suggest for King, my friend the comptroller of. . . . Oh, dear, no. He wouldn't do." (For he remembered in time that the comptroller really was a friend.)

"What nonsense is this from your lips?" demanded the King. "You? A raging man? Tush, Treasurer, tush. No one has a milder heart. However, so be it. You were about to suggest the comptroller of eminences. Send him in."

In he came. "Your Majesty loves his people too well, ever to make me King." The comptroller barely whispered it. "A fine King I would make, with my tantrums and distempers." "That was the treasurer's excuse," dryly remarked the other. The comptroller instantly changed his tune. "Furthermore, I am often ill with inner-head-pains. The incense a King must burn would sicken my head forever. But let me urge for your favor the master-of. . . . No. No. He is utterly unsuited." It is no nice thing to place a friend in the way of death. The comptroller remembered in time.

"You have worked every day for the last ten years," said the King to his comptroller of eminences. "Why didn't you tell me you were ill? But I thank you for reminding me of the master-of-pans. Send me that jolly fat cook, the scamp, for a talk, like yeast, to raise him."

If the cook had held a pan in his hand, he must surely have shaken many beans upon the picture carpet. Fortunately, he held no pan—only his willow-wood ladle. The chubby old chap had an oily voice. "Ho. Ho. Ho. So I'm to be King. Shen hao. Majesty would see fun in it if his crown were to melt upon his ears. But, Majesty, this I must tell you. I am a bad man. Just about the worst. I . . . I write poems, gamble at guess-fingers, steal from my little daughter's bank, and sometimes play at acting. Yes, I am bad. But don't feel disappointed. On the stage, nightly I see an actor, named Thang Jun. He is a grand person. He has a *way* with him. When he imitates a King, I'll vow I ask him if he'll have more rice. I think him Your Maj . . . I think him a real monarch. This man should be King. He has the voice, the bearing, and the eye."

"You refuse high office lightly," said the grumpy King. "Don't drip gravy on my newest robe. Send in all my officers—and go roast me a poem of a duck."

The chancellor was stout. The treasurer had a limp in his leg. The comptroller talked with a drawl. Now—this actor person, this Thang Jun, had mimicked all three. Moreover, he was far handsomer than the chancellor, more handsome than the treasurer, more than the comptroller. So. A very good time to have revenge. "An idea of excellence, Majesty," they said. "Put the actor on the throne. Give him the seal and the sceptre. Let the actor be our King." Even as he spoke, the chancellor felt of a letter in his sleeve. He well remembered the last line of that letter—"Will bring me a monarch's head." If a King, be he new or old, isn't a monarch, then no one is.

Two daughters the King had. Princess Pao Chu was beautiful. Princess Pomegranate Blossom could sing, she could sew, could embroider. To her the lute always gave its sweetest tone. She painted long-pictures and hung them upon the crumbling palace walls. But Princess Blossom was not beautiful. Neither was she ugly. Rather, say she was graceful.

The King spoke to his daughter, Blossom. "My child, you have heard of the whimsies of marriage fortune. A maid but seldom has the husband of her greatest love. I can't let you, my Daughter, marry Prince Ying." "I don't wish to marry Prince Ying," said the princess. She touched the silken many strings upon a lute, and sang of happiness.

"But, my dear, I must say further. You can't marry the duke."

"I'm happy for that. My wishes never turn to dukes," avowed the princess. The music from her lute affirmed that this was true.

"Nor the chancellor. You cannot marry him."

"Don't wish to. Never did. The chancellor is a very nice man, but not a one to marry."

The King, in his own way, had been leading up to what he feared would be cause for weeping. "You must marry Thang Jun, the actor." His daughter made no reply. But the silken strings were merry, and the song was still of happiness.

So Thang Jun married the Princess Blossom, but he was not at once a King. He was merely the husband of a princess. He was merely a problem for the King to study. The Ruler's old eyes were upon him. The cook and the chancellor reported every step he made.

The King inquired of his beautiful daughter, Pao Chu, "Child, does Thang Jun ever tell you of your loveliness?" "Of course not," said the unmarried princess. "He babbles for hours of the spirited way in which sister recites the Odes. I think *I* shall read a book."

The king, in his own way, had been leading up to what he feared would be cause for weeping.

"What?" exclaimed her father. "Is Thang Jun blind? Or, merely simple? But no matter. Does this son-in-law of mine complain because I allow him so little money?"

"No. No," said the princess. "He thinks of you with devotion. He is sorry he mimicked your walk upon the stage."

"What?" roared the King. "Mimicked my walk, eh." (He had many times been told he was stately.) "Now truly we have a great dunce in the palace. I'll teach him humility—upon the headsman's block."

Later, the testy old fellow remarked to Chancellor Wang, "This young man has no beard to his chin, it is true; yet the fault is not so highly serious. He has his merits. He can tell you a melon apart from a plum. And his daring can't be questioned. Let him take the throne and be King. Arrange for the ceremony of crown. . . ."

Entered the actor. "My royal father-in-law, will you give me permission to hunt wolves in the western plains? They are destroying your people." "Go, and have luck," said the King. "But don't stay too long." Then he whispered, "Chancellor, postpone the ceremony I spoke of. It seems I'll always have to be King."

In the west the skies were red by night

By day the west was overhung with smoke.
The enemy came slowly, taking his choice,
and burning all else.

Thang Jun, the one-time actor, drilled his
troops. On a level field he stood up two
dozen prime, large actors, dressed in blue.
A dozen smallish fellows, red bedizened,
leaped upon them. They had slapping-boards
for weapons. Slap. Slap. Slap. The
drums boomed a mild encouragement. Having fought a full five minutes, the red actors
yelled, "Help has come. Our Tiger Troops
are here." (One man had come to aid them.)
They screamed like the Shen of storms. The
drummers pounded frantically. And the
huge blue actors ran. All twenty-four, they
ran from the twelve and one.

"Now," said Thang Jun. "Twelve soldiers replace twelve red actors. You see
what an easy thing is war. One red man is
worth two blue. Fall into line. Strike them
hard. Oh, you musicians, drum me out a
battle-piece. Now. NOW. Fight." The red
soldiers rushed to victory. The actors, so
beaten and blue, ran away howling.

Soon the ancient red soldiers learned their parts without a fault. At the cue "Now. now," they grasped each man a queue, and belabored the foe. At the end of five minutes they chased the actors completely from the field. Thus the whole army was trained. The little red soldiers declared, "War is a pleasure. . . . We like it. A pleasure for us. . . . But—how we should hate to be the larger force, and wear blue uniforms."

Thang Jun himself led the army. On a barren plain he halted and ordered line of battle. His hatchetmen took station on the left flank. His battle-axe brigade formed the right. Bow-and-sword men occupied center and rear. While waiting, they practised to make their frowns more terrifying.

The giant general of the blue-clad foe approached. Thang Jun greeted him. "Have you eaten rice in pleasuring quantity? Your coat is the handsomest ever I saw." The blue general at once realized that he would need all his politeness. "My miserable coat would be scorned by a beggar. But you— *your* garments are beautiful. A pity it is

hang Jun replied, "Alas, I have no gold. I can't even pay
for the coat you have so admired."

they must receive my sword's cutting."
Thang Jun simulated sad surprise. "What!!
Distinguished Military Man must I really
believe you come in anger?" The enemy
leader said, "Oh, I'm not *very* angry. Bring
to my tent the five thousand catties of gold
and sign the peace. Let us escape this bitter
ness of battle." Thang Jun replied, "Alas
I have no gold. I can't even pay for the coa
you have so admired." "Then," declared th
blue foe general, "we must break sword:
When shall the battle be?"

Thang Jun, from the corner of his eye, ha
been watching blue soldiers manœuvre. H
saw blue donkey troops circling his flank. Ver
plainly, a trick. Therefore, instead of say
ing, "In half an hour"—the customary tim
—Thang Jun shouted, startlingly, "Nov
now. NOW." And "NOW" was the cu

The red troops bounded forward. Wha
clamor came from the drums. How th
swords flashed and fell. Steel upon irc
armor. Little red men with both hand
to their steel. BOOM. . . . CLASH. . .
CLANG. . . . BOOM. . . . WHANG. . .
WHACK.

Men fell, just as they had fallen on the play field. Some of them groaned and some did not. That was quite according to intructions. One minute, two minutes, another minute, four. The little red soldiers chuckled, "We are nearly through. One more minute, and the battle is won. Draw a full breath for the shouting."

The signal was given. Each red soldier shrieked like a demon. "Help has come. Our Tiger Troops are here." They dashed forward through the line. Utterly bewildered by such audacity, the blue-gowned foemen fled.

"War is easy," said the red soldiers. "Get up, imbeciles, you who were to play at being wounded. Why do you lie in the dust, when the signals say 'Arise'? Don't you know the battle is finished?" And the drums called and called, but many a man lay silent upon the plain of Han.

The aged King awoke from a game of chess with his chancellor. "Who's that coming? Is that my son?" "Yes, Majesty, your honored son." "Let's make him King tomorrow, Chancellor. The country is at peace, and the treasury well filled. We could select no better time." He turned and spoke to Thang Jun. "Was the wolf hunt successful? Where are the trophies of your never-failing bow? I've news for you, my son. Tomorrow, you'll be . . . you'll be. . . . What is it I wish to say, good Chancellor?"

THE KING WHO HAD NO DAUGHTER

In the merry Middle Kingdom a person tired sits to his rest in a carven chair; an upstanding, dragon-worked, proud, black chair. But, in the Eastern Island Land, which is Peng Lai, a weary one has no chair to sit in. That land is chairless.

Perhaps somebody will say to me, "Why is that? Why haven't they chairs in Peng Lai Land?"

I who write will tell you.

"Did they in Peng Lai never have chairs?"

I who write will tell you.

King Luan Khoo was in a sportive humor. He had a bowl of toasted melon seeds upon his royal lap. His pleasure was to nibble one seed and fillip the next at his chancellor. That was highly unfair, because the chancellor couldn't dream of filliping back at His Majesty. The melon seeds had come as a gift, with a letter from the Eastern Island Land. "What word shall I send him, Chancellor? Shall I answer him yes, or answer no? Answer me, yes, or no." But plainly, by his jollity, he knew which word he'd hear.

The chancellor put on larger spectacles, to give him a wiser face. "The word 'yes' has a pleasant look upon paper, Your Majesty. And remember, our treasury has forgot the feel of gold. The money in your treasure-hold wouldn't buy a bitten bean cake. We must be saving: and 'yes' requires less ink than 'no' to write." And that is perfectly true, in the written words of the Middle Kingdom. "Give him a 'yes,' Your Majesty, but be firm in the price I suggested. One man-weight of gold, color to be red."

The King objected, "But, Chancellor, it

just occurs to me: I *haven't* any daughter to let the Eastern Ruler have." The chancellor, wise as any whooing owl, was inclined to belittle, though craftily, the monarch's dearth of inspiration. "Wu Ta Lang, in lack of leather, cobbled his boots with melon rinds. There are so, oh, so many, very many maids in the world, Your Majesty, and who among them would refuse to be a king's adopted daughter?"

King Luan Khoo took very few minutes to see the point of this. He was delighted. "Oh. You mean that I . . . Shen hao (good). Clever Chancellor, clever idea. To show my appreciation, I shall pay your salary first of all, when the money arrives from Peng Lai. And more I'll do. I'll honor you by adopting *your* daughter; the prettiest one, Mee Lan." That was a blow unexpected, like a sword shaken down from a tree of plums. The chancellor remonstrated. "No, not my daughter, Your Majesty. Is war your wish? No. No. I mean you no violence." (The King had his hand on a sword.) "But consider, Majesty. My daughter is extremely ugly; and it's little the sign of a thinking head, to foist an ugly bride upon a prince. The Eastern Island men are ferocious in battle. They'd come under banners to Chang An City, and fight us out of the land."

But Luan Khoo had decided. "I have said. The sea is so constantly turned up by storms that I think few eastern war-men would live to cross it. Besides, I have my ten-thousand-tented brave army to make me bold. Mee Lan it shall be. With ink upon your writing brush make characters to fit my spoken words." Useless to argue. The chancellor wrote a letter, addressed to Prince Temmi Tenshi Ito San, at the palace, in Samisen, which city is in Mintoku, which is northernmost of Peng Lai, across the sea. "I take my pen in hand to write. . . ." (For that's a very ancient way to get a letter started. King Luan Khoo, himself, invented it.) "Excellent, Your Majesty. What next?"

"Mmmmmmm," said the King, already tired with thinking. "You can finish the

letter, Chancellor,—now that it's well begun.
I imagine I hear the comptroller of the four
eminences calling me, and it must be for
something important." So the King went out
to ride in a game of the exciting polo, and
his chancellor finished the letter.

Thus: *"and wish you pleasant rice. Your
Highness asks if my health is good? I answer 'Yes.' Your Highness asks if the
weather has been to my royal liking? I
answer 'Yes.' Your Highness asks if I'll
give him my daughter in marriage? I answer—'YES.' Oh, Great Prince of the
Islands Eastern, come upon a lucky day of
the calendar, and receive my daughter, Mee
Lan, in marriage. . . ."* ("Mee Lan won't like
this at all.") *"A gift, of course, you'll bring
me. . . . One man-weight, in gold. . . . I drop
the pen."*

The chancellor hastened with His Majesty's letter to the minister of foreign com-
munications. And a horse went out under
whip. And a postal boy was on the gone

horse, speeding to the east. By land, by minor streams and the rivers, by the violent waters of sea, King Luan Khoo's letter was speeded to the Isle Peng Lai.

Now is a very good time to state that the chancellor was a man often blessed with his moments of shrewdness. And daring—not half describes him. With the letter he had sent a picture . . . *not* of his daughter, the King's adopted daughter, Mee Lan . . . but, of the hideous witch old-hag, Hu Gung Seen. He thought, and had good reason for his thought, that nothing more would be heard of the marriage. A prince isn't likely to marry the very ugliest witch out of Kwen Lun Mountain. That's preposterous. To say it once more, the chancellor was shrewd. . . . But his own shrewdness was used against him.

The Eastern Island Prince sat on a mat of state, surrounded by his courtiers. "Speak freely," said he. "Don't fear for your heads. I left my sword in the tiring-room. Ha. The chamberlain laughs, and the commissioner of interior affairs puckers up in a grin.

But I am not offended. Laugh thoroughly. Here's a confession. . . . I, myself, was compelled to laugh when first I beheld this horrible portrait, this vinegar-grim, toad-ugly picture of the Middle Kingdom Princess."

The Eastern Island Prince sat on a mat of state, surrounded by his courtiers.

The chamberlain spoke. "Your Highness, I laughed, but not for what you may imagine. My laugh was wholly of appreciation, for I dearly love the little clevernesses that set a man above his fellows. In my youth I traveled through the Middle Kingdom. I know the customs of that land. The more beautiful a lady may be, the uglier she is

called, and uglier painted. Ho. Ho. Ho.
What an ugly picture. This thing is the
Chancellor Swom Djow's precaution. *He*
had the princess painted thus, and no demon
gazing on the paper would ever have desire
to steal the maid. The picture is ugliest I
have seen. Therefore, undoubtedly, the princess is in her superlative beauty. If Your
Highness is determined to marry an other-
land princess, let your bride be Mee Lan,
the incomparable, most beautiful maid in the
world. Marry Mee Lan."

"I," said the prince, with a last laughing
look at the portrait of Hu Gung Seen before
he hid it, face downward, under a scatter
rug, "shall." He called to the pages. "Get
my parade sword from the armory. Instruct
the master hostler to saddle a donkey train.
Tell my uncle to dress for the part,—he is
to rule while I am away."

A messenger came, riding in lather, to
Chang An City. "Prince Temmi Tenshi Ito
San is stepping from his sea-ship to the shore
rocks of Your Majesty's kingdom. The old
King chuckled. "Give him clear road. Order

the bandits to let him pass, undisturbed. If he's bringing the money, *I* want it all. I'll buy a new coat. I'll buy a new cow. I'll put my cat in sandals when the gold is mine."

Not long after came another spurring horseman. "Prince Temmi Tenshi Ito San rides in a witch's gallop. A hundred li he is, away, and the road mostly easy and downward." King Luan Khoo shouted orders. "Look to it, men, that the guns for salute are loaded full length. Sweep out the presence-chamber. Set a good table. There'll be red water-chestnuts, boiled in syrup, and my favorite Kwang Ting ducks. I'll want for the feast a profusion of gingered dumplings, potatoes out of the earth, and peaches down from a tree. Also, scallions. And clear the treasury of cobwebs."

The air was thick with cannon smoke, and incense. The odor of burning cedarwood, and baroos, and wood-of-sandal mingled with the sweetness of so hin blossoms, and flowers from the seven-furlong-fragrance tree. Players upon the scholar's-lute put forth noble music. They rivalled those who played the che of fifty strings. And the two-stringed violins were heard. And stout-armed fellows rubbed sticks down the musical-wooden-tiger's back. And there were drums.

Prince Temmi Tenshi Ito San seemed pleased with the wondrous greeting. When the music ran to the softer airs, he spoke to Luan Khoo. "You welcome me with lavish smoke and instrumentation, my very good friend the King. To say I am happy is not to say a moiety of what I feel. I brought you, as my first gift, a sack of la ya (salted dry ducks), because I have heard that you love them. What present do you hold for me?" The King thrust a finger toward a high, black chair. "A chair, Cousin Prince." (Of course, they were *not* cousins.) "My gift to you is a dozen of chairs carved with fighting dragons." (The old king's family was small. He could easily afford to give the chairs.) "We have heard that in your land the chair is unknown. So *I* give to *you*, and the chancellor gives to your courtiers, fine black chairs." "Oh, *excellent*," pronounced the Eastern Island Prince. "Now

I am pleased to the heart. Your kindness is engraven on my bones." He stooped to examine a prankishly chiseled dragon. And every courtier of his grasped a chosen chair, and voiced a word of pleasure.

King Luan Khoo invited, "Sit down, please, and rest the weariness out of you, while I go tell the cook to fan his fire. I know you are hungry and thinking of rice." He skipped through the door, anxious to see what delay had struck in the kitchen.

More than enough to worry him he found. The cook was furiously contemning the army, from general under peacock feather, down to the powder-boys. "Hung chang tung hsee. I'll resign for this. Those *don*keys, those *mon*keys of cannoneers, they took every coal of fire from my stove to light the guns, to salute the prince. And my kindling wood all wet." Woe in the kitchen. Very bad.

Meanwhile, in the presence-room, Prince Temmi Tenshi Ito San, feeling a lassitude, (alas that he did) tucked up his over-robe, and took to his chair.

And then . . . it happened, oh, shame that

it was. A wild out-flinging of hands, and a
shriek. A Cra-s-s-s-sh, as the chair went
down. And a Thu-u-u-u-mp. That was the
prince's body. And an "Ow-w-w-w-w-wh."
That was the prince's voice. Things had
come to a pretty pass, and *so they had*.
There lay the mightiest, the all-highest of
princes, the haughty Temmi Tenshi Ito San,
flat upon his back on the onyx floor. And it
was well, most fortunate, yea, that his groans
were loud and were frequent. Otherwise
there would have been tall business for the
headsman, for him who lops off heads with a
whickering sword; and the heads are impaled
on the castle wall. Because, a sound very
like unto laughter arose in far corners of the
room. The silly, the imbecile courtiers were
laughing at their prince. It is truth; there
were those of the prince's attendants who
giggled.

It cannot be denied, there *is* something
comic in the spectacle of an immense, a four-
hundred pound potentate falling through a
carven, weakly chair. It is funny to see a
mighty prince lying on the floor, arms and

There lay the mightiest, the all-highest of princes.

legs weaving the air, helpless to arise.
Admittedly it is laughable to hear a dig-
nified and prideful prince saying loudly,
"Oh-h-h-h-h-hh," in the tenor, "Ow-w-w-w-
w-wh," in bass. And the more distant attendants tittered. But not so with those
nearby. It was a matter serious and puzzling. Here lay the mighty prince in the dust,
dust, in the dust. And here were they, faithful to a man, anxious to aid, but unable.
Court etiquette forbade. It was against the
laws of their Eastern Realm for a person of
common clay to touch the prince. Not so
much as a little finger could they lay upon
him. And even had one of them the authority, he had not the requisite yama-mai silk
gloves. And the prince, all four-hundred
pounds of him, lay and groaned.

"Run," said a man of nimble thinking,
"to the chamberlain, who is coming on a
slower horse. He has the privilege of touch-
ing. He is a deputy minister-of-putting-upon-
the-feet." "We go. We go," said a dozen.
There was patter, patter, patter of stockinged
feet.

Some of the palace servants had learned of the tragedy. They came to do what they could. Drinks of sweetness and forget were placed beside the royal visitor. There was no rule against that. Thirty fan-bearers stood in a circle enclosing His Fallen Highness and eased him with their waftings. Again came players upon the melon-shaped guitar, and the sweeter, prohibit-all-fierceness lute. Flower maidens heaped so hin blossoms of rare perfume. They did what they could till the chamberlain arrived.

King Luan Khoo had heard nothing of the terrible catastrophe. At last, returning from the kitchen, he apologized for tardiness. "Forgive my cook for a lame right arm. Dinner won't be ready for an hour by the smoke-clock. While we are waiting, we might as well discuss the marriage. Of course you brought me the man-weight of gold???"

Prince Temmi Tenshi Ito San, on his feet, though trembling, put on a wan, small smile. "The money? No. I left it at home, for I feared a meeting with brigands. I'll write you an order on my treasury, and you may

send for the gold when you wish." King
Luan Khoo hid his disappointment with a
graceful sweep of the fan. "Exactly as I
had hoped. I doubt if there's a room for it
in my treasure vaults at present." (Oh, King,
how could you?) "But I'll find a place for
it; maybe out in a duck coop. Let's go into
the library, and write out the contract, and
affix the legal seals."

The King drew up a chair for his royal
guest. Temmi Tenshi Ito San quivered in
his body parts and trembled in his joints.
He dreaded to take the seat. But he couldn't
well save himself. It would never do to
refuse. So he sat in the chair. . . . And
nothing happened.

They handed him paper and the writing
brush. Luan Khoo himself ground ink—and
that is the highest compliment. The prince
wrote a contract of marriage between self
and the maiden Mee Lan. . . . "*In considera-
tion of which I undertake to give her father
the sum of——man-weight in gold.*" He
left a wide blank in front of man-weight
and that was crafty leaving. When all i:

said and all is done, one man-weight (picul)
of gold is a pretty penny. His Highness
intended to haggle. "What shall I write
here, Good Friend King? You said in your
letter, I think, one-half man-weight. But
your treasury is full, and the half would
embarrass you. Suppose I write one-third?"
He held his brush above the paper to write.
King Luan Khoo came close to argue. He
placed his hand on the prince's chair.

One too many straws in the burden will
send a camel to his knees. The weight of
Luan Khoo's hand on the chair was enough
to cause disaster. A splintering, crackling
sound arose. The chair went down in many
slivers. For the second time that day, His
Highness, Temmi Tenshi Ito San, knew the
hardness of the floor.

Fortunately the chamberlain, deputized to
couch, was in the room where needed. He
was a man of strength. Before a dozen
"Oh's" were uttered he had His Highness
standing.

With his old, sharp eyes the chancellor
peered; with his lean, sharp finger he pointed.

King Luan Khoo clutched the marriage contract. His face was an ivory sun of happiness. To the chancellor he whispered, "Prepare at once to make the journey. If they haven't the full seven in tzu chin (red gold), accept their silver—of equal value." To the prince he said, "A pleasing surprise is this, most honorable and gracious Highness. By the Blessed Hill called Tai, I had not expected such generosity. My gratitude is tinctured with the tears of happiness. SEVEN man-weight in gold."

His Highness suspected a trick. "What? Seven? Who? How? When? Where is the seven?" The King touched his gilded nail to the paper. And a 7 it was, written large.

Let me go back with the story, to explain the mysterious price. When the prince's chair splintered beneath him, his hands flew out, seeking support. They found it not, nothing remotely resembling support. But one of those royal hands still held the brush-that-talks-on-paper. And where His Highness had hesitated voluntarily to write the character for 1, his flying hand had involuntarily formed a large and exact 7.

Now seven was (and is), a mystic number, a Shen's number. Hence, when it was once written there was no erasing it, no withdrawing from the bargain.

Long did Temmi Tenshi Ito San gaze upon the paper. "It is, undoubtedly, a seven," said he. "And written by my own hand. What is done, is done. However . . ." he finished the sentence in talk to self, "I'll make passing sure that such a costly accident can never happen again. I may be in need of another wife some day, and I'll be happier in thinking that no chair in future can desolate my treasury. A demon's plague on chairs, anyhow." Forthwith and there, he sat on the floor and wrote a new law for his Eastern Islands. "Henceforth, let there be no chair, nor the equivalent thereof, in any way, shape or form, used in my City of Samisen. Nay, let there be no chairs in Hiuja, or Takekura, or in any place whatsoever or wheresoever in my Eastern Islands. *The penalty is understood.* Let there be no chairs."

I who write will say what happened next. The prince beckoned to his chamberlain. "Send this law to my islands, promptly. I wish it to be in effect when we return. Some of my courtiers, perhaps, will carry their gift chairs home; and, the raffish simpletons, I think I heard them giggle when their prince was in the dust upon the floor."

In another corner, the chancellor wailed privately to his monarch, Luan Khoo. "Oh, Majesty, trouble is upon us. The whole world's gone a-wrong. Bad. Bad, to the full extent of the word. Terrible. Terrible, worse than that. My daughter, *your* daughter, little Mee Lan, has eloped with the treasurer's son." The King had little to say to that, but such as it was he said it. "My word," and he went to his bed-and-slumber room and prepared for an ache of the head.

Mee Lan was safe away from the city. The prince went home, cross as two sticks, brideless, and tearing the contract into pieces of little size. Of course, he saved his money. The seven man-weights of gold remained in the island treasury. But the law in respect to chairs was pasted in the statute books as written. Peng Lai is a chairless land.

The ink's gone dry. *Cha bah doah.* I who write have told it.

LITTLE BROTHER

First came Wing,—the eldest,—Wing the giant-heighted. He was tallest of the brothers who were three. It isn't too much of too much to say that he was tallest of the tall. Not once shall I state Wing's size in figures out of arithmetic books. Because—I have a reputation for truth-telling, and become sad when persons murmur, in derisive accent, shoulders shrugging, "*Ten fiddlesticks*." But, Wing was tall . . . with straightest lips I do assure you.

Ming was the second brother. Ming was medium. Ming had only an everyday height. But at that, he was much, much taller than Brother Sing. Sing, undoubtedly, was small. Wing and Ming usually called him "Little Brother." Sometimes they named him "Little Sing," but that's too much like baby talk.

To see Little Brother so small, constantly grieved the elder two. He was old enough, they thought, to come above the table. They sorrowed increasingly. Said Ming to Wing, "Little Brother'll be a dwarf if we don't have a care. Let's feed him such food as the Witch Giants eat . . . that's sesame and coriander." Wing remonstrated, "We have no money buried in the flooring, nothing of a silver gleam hidden under the eaves. Sesame is sold, not given. Yet, we *must* make Little Brother get tall. Here's a plan. I'll take his ears, and you take his toes. You pull, and I'll pull. We'll stretch Little Brother."

Ming had a poor opinion of the plan. "You don't know your strength, Elder Brother. It's the most enormous ever had by a man in all the country round. Why,

you'd pull Little Brother in two thin pieces.
My scheme is much better I'm thinking. Oh,
yes, it is. The sun makes bamboo grow, and
mustard. Let's stand Little Brother in the
sunlight. Put him in the sun and watch him
grow."

So every day they stood Little Brother
where the sun shone brightest. They had a
short yardstick by which to measure. "Any
growth, Brother?" "Not even an inch." "Oh,
dear. And there wasn't a cloud in the sky."
Every day they made the same complaint.
Poor Little Brother stood still in height. He
was nicely browned, but he took no growth.

Said Wing to Ming, "I hate to seem un-
brotherly, yet I must say these words. I
work and you work. Little Brother does
nothing at all of gainful nature. Is that
proper? Why shouldn't Little Brother earn
money to pay for his rice and the bean cake
he loves so well? He should help in the
upkeep of our house." Ming said, "That, I
am persuaded, has the sound of truth. Our
wealth is gone and our table bare. Little
Brother should help us fill the rice boiler."

Forthwith they arranged it. Little Brother must toil for his dolichos and scallions, or go hungry.

In those days a man must find work as best he could. He couldn't write in a paper, "I want work," and see merchants, lawyers, master-smiths trooping to his door. He had to go seek. Little Brother, Little Sing, went to the field of a farmer. He bowed deeply and spoke humbly. "Honorable rich farmer, I am a workman looking for work. I can do much in the way of toil." (He looked it. As high as the farmer's waist.) "I undertake that my spade shall grow no rust. Kindly tell me what I'm to do."

The farmer laughed explosively. "Ho, ho, ho. Ho, ho, ho. Ho, ho." He looked at Little Brother as he laughed, and Little Brother grew offended. "I know my robe is many-patched, but why should that amuse you? I'll go elsewhere to work in a field."

Holding his head high, he went to another farmer. "Beneficent farmer, I am a chore-man, looking for work. Hire me, and I'll be the best choreman ever in your cabbages.

No doubt from time to time you'll give me praise." The farmer spread his toothless mouth. "He, he, he. He, he, he. He, he." Little Brother let temper guide his tongue. "I know my girdle is made of hemp, but is that a reason for coarse laughter? I shall let some other man employ me."

He rambled and rambled, and always heard rude merriment. A whole day's walking gained him no work. The farmers didn't seem to need a workman. Silly louts. What loud laughter they made. Little Brother went home and told his tale. "I heard men in foolish laughter, but no one said 'Work.' They called me Toad-in-a-coat." He ate bean cakes with fury.

Brother Wing said, "Let me *fan pai yen*." (Turn up a white eye. That means "to think.") He set his chin in the palm of his hand. Brother Ming said, "Think. And I'll think too, for good measure." He put his head on the table and closed his rolling eyes. At bed time Brother Wing exclaimed "Hao. Think no more, my medium brother. I have a plan for tomorrow's use. Put the round

bamboo beneath your pillow-bone and sleep."
But Ming was already asleep.

In the morning, in the dew time, Brother
Wing walked far. Wing passed by the little
farms. Little farms in that land hire few
workers. When he came to a large field with
only one man in it, he left the road and
walked a furrow. "Honorable farmer," said
Wing the tremendous, in a little voice, "I
wish you the five happinesses. May you
always have peach trees to keep the ghosts
away. Prosperous landholder, gaze at my
hands. They are hard. View my shoulders.
They are broad. Have you any lifting for
such shoulders, any spading for such hands?"
The farmer squinted upward to the one who
over-shadowed him. His mouth fell open.
"Esteemed Large Person, come out of your
robe. Here are potatoes to be removed from
earth. I'll pay you well, and feed you better.
By the village blue idol you've the size for
a worker. A giant, or larger." How the
potatoes came up from the soil. The donkey
who carried them off was saddened. Brother
Wing was a willing spade-man. He earned

Brother Wing was a willing spademan.

twice over every coin he threaded on his cash rope.

Next day, exactly as planned, Brother Ming—Ming, you will note, went to the farm and threw out potatoes. Now Ming was the medium brother. His face was the face of Wing, but his form was quite his own. At once the farmer squinted and said, "How is this? Yesterday you were large. Today you are only medium. Witch changes always frighten me." Ming replied, "That's easily explained. Yesterday I wore high boots. Today I wear shoes." Which was quite true. Absolutely. Nevertheless, the farmer was still puzzled. "But your shoulders, man. Did they shrink in the rain? They are not so broad as they were." Brother Ming had prepared for any question. "My shoulders always look smaller under tight cloth. I wear a closely fitted coat today." Up came potatoes by bushels and pecks. The donkey groaned and felt grieved that ever he had been born to carry burdens. Brother Ming was a worker of excellence. He earned far more than the money he bore home on his cash string.

Next day—and this had been carefully planned from the beginning—who should go to the farm but one named Sing,—Sing, better known as Little Brother. He put his hands to the work. The air was filled with potatoes. But when the farmer caught sight of Little Brother, then a farmer nearly thought to pray. "Confusion," cried the man-of-the-field. "Honorable workman, are you a magician? What have you done with your height?" Little Brother had been thoroughly coached in the words he should use. "Yesterday I wore shoes. Today I am footed with sandals." That was no blemish upon his lips. He told the truth, from Y to the end. The worried farmer said, "Well, let me beseech you, don't come tomorrow with feet worn bare. I'll not be able to see you in the furrow." Little Brother, busily unearthing potatoes, promised to come with feet covered. The donkey groaned. Master Sing was no sluggard. He treated his work as something to be done. He earned every cash that went home on his shoulder.

A strolling scholar came to the house one

evening, in a fall of rain. This was to the
house of Wing and Ming and Little Brother.
The scholar wished a cover for the night.
"Honorable Householder, can you spare me
space at the fire? The winds of storm are
running free. I wear a scholar's coat, thin
and unprotective in such a lash of rain."
"Plenty of space. Step in," said Wing.
"We have it dry under our thatched roof."
The scholar knew pleasant words to say.
"My gratitude shall last a thousand years.
What an elegant palace you own. Such nice
red earth for floor. And your pig is handsome. Tonight I shall read to you from
my books, for undoubtedly you are interested
in the classics. But first I must eat. Long
on the road has given me a hunger."

Wing called to Little Brother. "Put the
scholar's name in the rice kettle." And to
the visitor he said. "Here is a chair close
to the table. What is your high sounding
name, and what your road?" The scholar
replied, "My hardly-worth-mentioning name
is Thang Toy. I'm out of the land of Kiang
Theen. My road leads to the Capital City,

where I am to take the last examination. I shall receive the *tsin sze* degree (Complete Scholar), and be powerful and respected. Learning is a wonderful thing, householder. Today I plead for food and a mat on which to ease my bones. A month from now I'll be a governor. I'll wear a pictured robe—shower-of-roses silk." (Wing's eyes had begun to pop. He motioned Little Brother to put on another kettle.) "Think of my wealth to come, householder, and rejoice with me. My poor old father begs in a ditch, unable to secure work. He is a carpenter. In a little while all men will say to him, 'Honorable Thang Yin, will you not build my coffin? Name your own price. What health has your son the governor?' And this will come to pass, muscular householder, because of my learning and office."

Wing said, "Explain to me more fully Use simple words, noted scholar. I have heard of this matter you call 'learning' and wish to understand better what it is." The willing scholar smiled and talked an hour

Brother Wing's mouth was open the entire while. Brother Ming kept a hand behind his ear. Little Brother minded the kettles.

As they ate evening rice, Brother Wing put questions. "When is the moon closest to earth?" That was one. The scholar gave his opinion. Wing said, "I thought as much. My nails are short (scholars' nails are long), but you see I can think. Now answer me, which is the farther from here, Chang An City, or the shining sun?" The scholar blinked and hemmed and hawed. "A-hem," said he, "that is a question for loud dispute. I've heard it before, but the page it is on was torn out of my book. Have you an ink slab and a writing brush, and a calculating board?" Little Brother laid his "nimble boys," his chop sticks, aside. "I can answer that. The sun is farther than Chang An City. We often see men from Chang An, but who has seen a man from the sun?"

"Marvelous," exclaimed the guest. "Are you a graduate? Dear, dear, how you must have laughed at my ignorance. What meaning do you read from 'The wrinkled waters have no grief'? My teachers differed in their explanations."

Little Brother blushed. "I am no graduate. I spoke in fun, and not from knowledge. Chang An is farther than the sun. We can see the sun; but climb the highest hill in this region and we can't see Chang An City."

"Extraordinary," gasped the scholar. "If you are not a graduate it is because you haven't taken the examinations. May a flame singe my beard, you're a better scholar today than I'll be in my nineties." Thereafter he boasted far less of his learnedness.

When the scholar had gone his road, eldest brother Wing said to second brother Ming, "You heard what the scholar remarked about learning. Learning will not only benefit him, but his sons, and his father, and brothers, and sisters. Let us make a scholar of Little Brother. I have a large head, yes, and so had Wu Ta Lang. You can't remember 'cat.' Neither of us could be scholars, but Little Brother can. We'll have only to work a bit harder the next few years. When Little Brother graduates and takes his grand high office we'll soon be repaid for our trouble. We'll both of us go through life like princes, done up in silks, and drinking first-bud tea. I've always longed to taste it."

Brother Ming replied, "How did my own secret thoughts get upon your tongue, Brother Wing? That's exactly the scheme I was turning. First a scholar, then a governor, then perhaps guardian of the four eminences. Come here, Little Brother. There's news to be told."

Now this is what Little Brother said to the farmer. "Honorable Farmer, I wish to be a scholar. I must read books, instead of burrowing like a mole in potato fields. A scholar can't study when weary. Please, if you're kind, release me from the agreement between us two."

The farmer answered, "Well of all things, of all Sings. You wish to break the contract, eh? Now that I've taught you to work. Oh, no. Serve through the year, and then you may scholar it all you please." Little

Brother blustered, "If you don't let me go I'll grow smaller." The farmer merely laughed. *"Grow* smaller." "If you don't let me go I'll grow larger." "Then *grow* larger," said the farmer. "A little larger would improve your work." Master Sing stayed at his digging all the day, and how he was furious.

Next morning Brother Ming, Ming the Medium, worked amid potatoes. The farmer squinted an eye and chuckled. "You must be a wizard's son. You've grown to twice your size in a night." Ming replied, "Oh, no. I'm quite ordinary, though I do think I'd make a fair scholar. Cold weather is coming so I've put on my shoes. Therefore you think I am taller." The farmer was merry all morning. Ming did a tremendous amount of work.

But all afternoon the farmer was glum. He talked to himself in terms of vegetables. "Ten catties of rice. A bushel, at least, of potatoes. Pears, I should say several dozen. A peck of scallions. Mutton (though strictly speaking that is not a vegetable). Melons, cabbage, and apricots, why the man ate enough for a tailor's whole family." But his workman pranced and sang, "The scholar read his book a-wrong, a sad mistake but a merry song." "I feel like I'm growing still larger," said Ming.

Next morning Big Brother Wing took a turn in the potato field. The farmer blew out his breath. "Whew-w-w. You certainly know the trick of growing." Then he mumbled to himself, "I dread the time when you put elbows on my table." Wing explained his extra size. "Boots, Honorable Farmer, hob boots. I'm a person of warmth-loving toes. My boots make me look quite tall. Has the sun gone noon? I'm working up a hunger." Many times that morning he asked, because he knew it made the farmer writhe, "Has the sun reached middle sky? Hungry's a terrible feeling."

Just as the farmer feared, so did sorrow gripe him. He moaned and beat his breast. He could eat no dinner. The time was taken in carrying rice. He and his wife carried kettlesful and cauldrons. Wing emptied the table and politely asked for more. It was too, too much. The farmer wiped his moist brow and smiled feebly. "Dear Sing (but it was Wing, all the time), I was jesting when I said you couldn't go. Never shall it be said that *I* stood in the way of great learning. I gladly burn our contract. Go and be a scholar, and remember your old friend the farmer when you get to be a governor." ("*Ai yu.* He ate more rice than my whole new crop will give.")

Little Brother bought him spectacles and books and candles. His new task was a joy. He had a memory like *lac*. Say "thirty-seven thousand one o three" to Little Brother in June of the year, and he'd recall it New Year's Day. To the singing of his kettle he recited all the odes. The odes rhyme, to be sure, in the old style pronunciation, but even so there's a chance to slip. The Book of Changes is written without any rhyme, written, like so many books, maliciously planned to bewilder us. No matter. Ask Little Brother for page forty-three, and he'd name every word without falter. He bought good

candles and used them well. By and by the
house was lonely for a week. Little Brother

Little Brother bought him spectacles and books and candles.

had gone to take the Budding Talent examination. That's the first and easiest.

Big Brother Wing worked for a man of
great hardness, a man seldom seen to smile,
never known to give an extra cash, sparing

with pleasant words. Greatly surprised was Wing, peacocked up with pride, when the master said, "I don't wish to seem rudely over-urgent, but will you kindly accept more money for the enormous work you do in my shop? Why do you not call socially at my miserable hut? I shall tell the cook to boil a double kettle for first-leaf tea tonight." Later that day Wing heard that Little Sing had passed the first degree. Neighbors for miles around came in with congratulations. They brought presents.

But Little Brother had far to go. Budding Talent is very fine, but Budding Talent is never made governor. There's *ku jen* (Exalted Man) yet to be striven for. And there's *tsin sze* (Complete Scholar) to be won. It is the hardest. Never try for that degree unless your mind can stand all hardships. During examination at least a dozen men become utterly insane.

Little Brother went through his books. They were never far from his thought. At the table,—and they had a queer way at table to eat the rice—Big Brother always knelt,

medium Ming sat in a chair, and Little
Brother stood—at the table Little Sing was
like as not to say, "Have more bean curd,
Brother Wing. Saith sage and scholar Choo

At the table—and they had a queer way at table to eat the
rice—Big Brother always knelt, Medium Ming sat in a chair,
and Little Brother stood—

Tze, 'A circle of the Vast Extreme (the
heavens) is merely a straight long line. In
other words, a line drawn far becomes a
circle.' Dolichos, Brother Ming. 'In the
Vast Extreme, a circle.' But never mind
the circles. Have a dish of scallions."

Even Wing got into the ways of the scholars. It was ridiculous to hear the big fellow recite "The caterpillar said to the moth." He would take Little Brother upon his knee for hours and repeat the learning.

Little Brother passed the second degree.

And the days passed. Weeks passed. And a year. Many a candle had drowned in its own fat. Study. Study. Late and early, Little Brother had studied. The time was near for reward.

Big Brother Wing spoke to medium Ming. "*A ta jen* (great man) is coming. Hear the sedan bearers chant in the road." Ming replied, "Some one from the capital in that chair. I know his city by the song." The chair went by in dust. Sang the front carriers, a word for each foot put down,

> "*Lah hung he*
> *Kee lah hung*
> *Lah lung hah*
> *Kee luh lung.*"

Then the rear men took the tune "They've stopped their travel," said Ming

"They're coming back," said Wing. The man who came in the chair inquired, "Is this the tall house of Sing the graduate? Very well, knock your heads. I who sit here am the Chief Examiner. Runners notify the ordinary graduates, but such men as take notable honors I notify in person. Oh, yes, and here is the red letter of appointment. Graduate Sing is to be Prefect."

"What shall we do?" asked Wing of Ming. "What shall we do?" asked Ming of Wing. "Who'll wake us in the mornings?" That was Wing. "Who'll tell us pretty stories?" That was Ming. "Who'll trim the candles?" Wing speaking. "Who'll take the lark in his cage for an airing?" Ming speaking. "We are content with things as they are. Why can't we have tomorrow, as days have been in the past? Do you think we can let him leave us? Can we let Little Brother go?" They thought until the candle ate its wick. Said the sorrowful Wing, "Let us enter our beds, Middle Brother, and dream of what's to be done."

And *then* what happened? I who write

don't know. But I notice in History that a man named Sing was thirty years governor of Hiang Chwan. He was only so tall, says History.

THE WAS-A-BOY

Sueh Chung, the honorable farmer, dwelt near Seang Tsoo, village of one small temple, and less than a dozen fires. That place is only three li the other side of Cherry Bloom Hill, though geographies make it look farther. Sueh Chung had land—I've said he was a farmer. Sueh Chung had a donkey, four ducks, and a son, together with necessary buildings and fruit bushes. His land measured six *mou*, say an acre, and that will be right. It was fertile land. Only the strong could lift a melon. It was liberal land, a perfect mine for potatoes. The hungry could do shallow digging anywhere and fetch up a dinner. A good farm.

The donkey pulled with great steadiness and strength at the end of a plow. He carried heavy burdens in haste. Furthermore, he was easy on shoes. A good donkey.

The ducks were decorative and profitable. They fished their food from the river, and buyers never complained that their eggs were unlucky. Good ducks.

The farmer's son moves in and out of the story, so there's no need to describe him.

One day in the time of harvest, Sueh Chung filled two baskets with garden goods and fastened them upon the donkey's sides. He said to his son, "Ah Yit, take these ground-eggs, and peas, and few radishes, to the market place and sell them. They are good potatoes, so rich they can be fried in their own fat. The market men should smile and count out money for half an hour. When you have sold the potatoes, go to the potter market and buy three large crocks and a vinegar jug. But above all, do not beat the donkey, because brittle-ware dislikes great speed. And watch your peas and queues." (A boy wears two queues—one each side of his head.) Ah Yit answered, "Very well, Severe One (two words for father), I'll leave my bamboo at home. Then the donkey will go slow footed, and the brittle-ware will keep its shape all the way from market." He caught the donkey's leading rope. *"Lai la* (come). Come with me, slow bones, and carry the potatoes to market." The donkey, of course, made no reply. He obeyed the pull on his neck and went along so smoothly he barely stirred a dust. All was well, for a time, all well and the goose hung high, though there really wasn't any goose, only potatoes, peas, and weigh-a-pound radishes. Ah Yit led and the donkey followed, and there was no hint of disaster to come.

The first person to be met was Lin Ah Juy. Lin Ah Juy was a lover of do-nothing. He enticed Ah Yit to dally. "Your donkey looks ready to fall in the road. Why do you

not give him a rest to cure his weariness?
Let us sit in the shade and play *tsooey
mooey*, while he recovers his strength."
"We've traveled only one li," said Ah Yit,
"and a li is nothing tiresome. However, I
haven't played guess-fingers once today.
Rest, donkey. Play, Ah Juy. Seven Change-
ables. Eight Shen. What? Are you cheating already? You did. You didn't. Do
you think my eyes are covered with road
stones for spectacles?" They played the
game guess-fingers in the usual way, with
loud shouts and constant squabbling, but in
perfect good humor.

The donkey had been tied to a tree. He
didn't stay tied for long. That donkey knew
what could be done with teeth and common
sense. He worked the rope loose and wandered down the road to nibble. "Three
Firsts. Six Directions. Nine Dragons. Five
Sons." The donkey soon disappeared.

Here, some people undoubtedly will say
"We know what happened. A train of ban
dits came along and stole the donkey, o
perhaps only the potatoes. Then Ah Yi

went home, and the Severe One broke a bamboo." But such was not the adventure. Late in the day Ah Yit remembered what he had

He played the game guess fingers in the usual way.

to do. He said, "Chin, Chin," to Lin Ah Juy, and found the donkey. And he scolded the donkey, "Get along faster, you creature of pokiness. Are you going to dawdle all day? *Tsew. Tsew*" (Go on). He caused the donkey to run, while he followed close behind, constantly suggesting more speed. They had a long and difficult hill to climb. There were rocks in the road, knee high, and many of them. But the donkey skipped 'round and over, and no harm fell till the hill top was reached. There the little beast stepped on his rope and went down, head and ears. Some of the potatoes flew in one direction, and many in another. Ah Yit felt moved to speak his wrath. The donkey's fault, of course. "Now look what you've done, Sinful. Here's a potato broken. Here's one utterly mashed. How filled with wickedness you are; like a *poom* for misbehavior."

A little house stood on the hill top. Hens were in its yard. These hens imagined great luck had come their way. They went at Ah Yit's scattered potatoes and began to dine. The boy promptly quit scolding his donkey and turned to the fowls. He picked up stones. "Have I not enough trouble, without your adding to it? Chut, you thieves. I'll make you fit to receive your completed names." Now, a man's completed name is given him in his coffin. He's dead. It may be that a fowl's completed name is given it in the kettle. However that may be, in noisy disorder the hens ran off and scuttled under the house. But Ah Yit continued to throw stones. Some broke tiles on the roof, and one went through the paper of a window. Out came an old man in a clear red coat. It was red; it wasn't blue. This wearer of the red coat had the look of a thousand years. His voice was unsteady. He was sorry his hens had crossed the road. "I shall denounce them thoroughly, younger brother, later. But now I must help you pick up your potatoes. Such wicked fowls. These have been fine potatoes. Terrible hens, very bad. I've seldom seen better. (Potatoes, probably, he meant.) The rascals, they'll smart for their misdeeds."

But Ah Yit was not to be soothed by language, neither by the aid received. "The fowls ruined many potatoes," he declared. "You must pay me twenty, yes all of thirty cash for the damage." The old man probably thought it only just. He paid without argument. Then he finished filling baskets, and tied the donkey's rope out of reach of a hoof. Ah Yit soon shouted his *"Tsew. Tsew,"* and the donkey went off at his best.

At the market place Ah Yit met new worry. The stony-hearted buying man appeared to be sad because such potatoes were offered him. He said, "These potatoes have been mistreated. They are bruised and broken, and I can think of many other faults. No cook would own them, but perhaps I can sell them to some poor man who wishes to make *sam shu* and be drunken. I'll give you far too much, one hundred cash." Ah Yit whined, "Of course they are crushed, because a villainous old fellow in a red coat on the hill threw them too heavily into the baskets. If you won't pay more than one hundred cash, then a hundred cash is all I'll get. But dear oh, me, it is very little. These potatoes are almost honey."

The man would say no higher price, so Ah Yit took the money and bought pottery, as his father had instructed. The coins he carried on his homeward trip made a very light burden. He knew his father would be disappointed. There was a chance that the Severe One would scold. So Ah Yit thought of a plan to get more copper. He decided to make the red-coated man of the hill-top house pay another ten cash for damage done by his hens and himself. While the thought was hot in Ah Yit's mind, he struck the donkey and told him to trot.

Possibly some persons will say, "Oh, yes, we know what happened. Ah Yit disregarded his father's advice, and trotted the donkey, and thereby a crock and three vinegar jugs were broken. *Cha lah doah*." But that is not quite the way things happened. Night had come. It lacked a moon, and the stars were far away. The donkey was hustled along at such a pace he was oftener off the crooked road than on it. In consequence he went where it was trespassing to go. Presently he leaped to one side and stopped. A man groaned, "Oh-h-h." In a cracked voice he said, "Pardon me very much for stopping your donkey. I thought you would travel the road, not through my cabbage garden. It was perfectly silly of me, and I am sorry."

Ah Yit spoke angrily. "A-ha. You are the old man on the hill with the hens. I want more money. You've frightened my donkey and shivered my brittle-ware. Now you'll pay for it." "Eh? What's that?" the old man exclaimed. "Then you are the young gentleman who lost his potatoes, and stoned my property, both house and hens. Come to the door where a light is, and I can see to count money." In a minute he opened his door and let the light shine upon Ah Yit. "Now," said the householder, "you shall have your due. I, in my time, had a hand for magic. If the charm works, your ears will twitch." He made motions with a fan, and threw a smoking powder in the air. (Sure enough, Ah Yit's ears began to twitch.) "Now I shall count. *Yih, urh, san.* Shen be kindly. *Sze, woo, luk.* Hear my wish. Seah." (Seven is the magic number.) "Let the change appear."

Ah Yit's ears grew long and his feet grew hard. He tried to speak but could say only

He made motions with a fan, and threw smoking powder in the air.

"Onkey." And he hung his head, for the bridle was heavy. He who had been a boy, was now a donkey. And, more of the magic, that which had been a donkey—was now a boy. The old magician of the hill had changed the two of them.

The hairy, four-legged was-a-boy again said "Onkey." The two-legged now-a-boy (the once-a-donkey), blinked and gazed curiously down at the coat upon him. He said, "It was dark and I didn't see your cabbage patch. Please forgive me for breaking any." He turned and led the was-a-boy away.

After a while the old man of Cherry Bloom Hill remembered a thing he had forgotten. He said to himself, "Dear oh me. The now-a-boy will have a sad time when he gets home." He went to the roadside and whooped to be heard at a distance. "Boy. Boy. Now-a-boy." But the now-a-boy was gone through the forest. And the old man chided himself. "I should have put money in his girdle purse. The farmer may be angry and dispraise him. It's plain as a Kiang Sing toad that I'm getting too old and forgetful to do my magic according to book."

When Now-a-boy reached home the farmer said, "Supper is ready, my son. Sit at the table, and while you eat tell me what luck in your trading. Is this all the money you brought?" Now-a-boy regarded a pickled egg and seemed to find it a curiosity. "I did the best I could, Master-Daddy, but you see I fell down, and all the potatoes tumbled from my back. Then the old man opened the door, and the boy said 'Very bad hens.' Both picked potatoes and I ate grass. There's mighty good clover a-top the hill. Then we went to market, and here I am. But it isn't so clear on my tongue as it is in my mind." The farmer was uneasy. He said, "My poor son, you are ill, and incoherent. Don't worry about the money. Go to bed, and I'll soon have the doctor in to give you charred tiger's bones, to be followed by bees' honey."

A man came to buy the farmer's donkey, to buy the was-a-boy. The farmer said, "I am willing to sell, for a good price, but mind you, it must be good. My donkey is a doer of great deeds in harness. And he's plump as a bacon pig." The man was inclined to haggle. "A good price deserves a good donkey. Will you break a saucer and say this donkey is well set up and able? What is wrong with his eyes?" Large tears were rolling down the donkey's cheeks. The farmer vowed, "He never cried before. He is intelligent and hears us talking of his sale." The worthy buyer, I suppose he was worthy, remarked, "That may be. But before I buy I must put a saddle on him and ride rapidly a mile. Why, what on earth is wrong with him now?" The was-a-boy galloped to the house. He galloped straight through the door. He was on his knees and half under a bed when his master and the dealer entered. The dealer declared, "That donkey is bewitched, or bedemoned, or something of the sort. Really, I shouldn't care to own him." The farmer's surprise was evidenced in quick sentences. "My word. My stars. My goodness. He never acted like this before. But anyway, I sha'n't sell him." The was-a-boy said his thanks with "Onkey. Onkey. Onkey."

Ah Yit, the now-a-boy, worked very hard. He was the easiest person in the land to get out of bed on a morning. There was no rooster in the farmhouse to waken him, but he always arose when the ducks quacked. At night he had to be told it was bed time, seemed perfectly willing to toil all night. Once Sueh Chung said to him, "My son, the sleeping-room floor is in need of new matting. Go upon your pair of stoutest legs to the marsh-land and gather rushes. I'll teach you how to weave a mat." Ah Yit answered, "I cut rushes yesterday, and the mat is half woven." The farmer shook his head, and continued to shake it as long as he spoke. "A great change has come over you, Ah Yit. Of old you were often unwilling. Now you do things without being told. It isn't natural. You work hard and are becoming thin. Never mind the rushes; let us go and fly our kites. You, Ah Yit, take the belled red kite, and I, Sueh Chung, will have the yellow one with the whistle. Make a noise, Ah Yit. Dear,

Make a noise, Ah Yit. Dear, dear, you're not as much boy as
your father is.

dear, you're not as much boy as your father is."

It was the time of short days and long nights. Ah Yit said to the stern one, "This is cold weather, and I pity our donkey. I go to the forest and get leaves for his bed. He wears my old coat of a night. I do what I can but I know he is cold. The stable lets every wind sweep through. Please, may I build a new house for the donkey?" Sueh Chung at once gave consent. "By all means do. A feeling comes to me that the donkey is one of our family. I'll help you in the work." So they made an excellent dwelling for the donkey; it was next to the farmhouse kitchen, cosy and warm.

For a long time the donkey, the was-a-boy, felt disinclined to carry weights or pull the plow. Sueh Chung often said, "I intend to beat this stubborn lazy-one, some day when a stick falls in my hand." Every time he said that the was-a-boy wept. Sueh Chung had only ordinary patience. But Ah Yit had the mildness of a wooden idol. He coaxed the donkey and cajoled him. By and by the was-a-boy became a good worker.

Each time Ah Yit went to market the old
man of Cherry Bloom Hill had something to
say. "How does your donkey do? Is his
temper sweet? Does he work with a will?"
Ah Yit always answered, "He is a *good* one.
He gets better every day. We could sell him
for a handsome price but no in*deed* we
won't." And the old man always finished,
"You, yourself, work much harder than you
should. You are thin as a seedling growing
in shade of the banyan tree. Mix your work
with play."

But Ah Yit was sober-sided. It was seldom he had a feeling for fun. He would
run and jump, but there his playing stopped.
To make a top, or to spin it, he thought a
waste of time.

The old man of Cherry Bloom Hill shook
his gray head more and more. In his talks
with himself it was a daily habit to say, "The
now-a-boy takes life too seriously. If things
continue as they are he will not live long.
When the signs are proper I must do what
can for him. It is my duty, perhaps my
bounden duty. Eagles for the side of heaven

fishes for the sea. Donkeys for the grassy ways, and boys for play. To change them is not good."

At last one night when the sky was as black as it ever can get, and the owls called constantly each to each, the old man read in his musty books and announced with finality, "This is the night and the hour. Witches are saying their '*Om mi to fo*' (Prayer), saying it backward, their '*Om mi to fo*.' The sign of *woo* meets the sign of the great Shen. *Hao*. It is good. I shall up with me and go, go to the farmstead of Sueh Chung, and the changes I make will be changes of good."

Sueh Chung, with big square spectacles to help his eyes, sat reading the almanac (I nearly spelled it with a k). Sueh Chung was a farmer, and your farmer, above all men, must keep informed of almanack knowledge. He turned to Ah Yit and said, "After to-morrow and another clear day we shall have rain. The spots on the picture cow in the book foretell great changes, and the reading is, 'A wise man's umbrella stays close to his hand.' I take it that means rain." Ah Yit said, "I'm glad you told me of what's to come. Tomorrow I shall put new tiles where needed on the roof." Sueh Chung read more and changed his opinion. "The rain may not come after all. The next line raises a doubt." He raised his own eyes. . . . "My word. My stars. My goodness, my donkey, what are you doing in here?"

His donkey stood upon the kitchen floor. "Well. Well. Well," from the farmer. "I can't imagine how you got in, but since you *are* in, you might as well stay. No doubt you were cold in the stable."

It now occurred to Sueh Chung that he was hearing unusual noises, which seemed to come from the stable. Hastily he grasped his instead-of-the-moon (lantern), and a great stick. "Demons, undoubtedly," thought the farmer. But he wore a wristlet of carven peach stones. He wasn't afraid of however many demons. He unlocked the stable door.

A strong wind snuffed his lantern light. Laughter was heard in the donkey stall. And then a voice saying, "Honorable Daddy, yo

played me a trick, fastened me in the stable.
I was asleep and you locked me in."

The magic had worked. *Cha bah doah.*
Donkey was donkey, and boy was boy. And
each was all the better.

THE WIND THAT WOULDN'T BLOW

HAI PONG, the Wise Man, received a lette
from his King. Having lighted a tree-o
lamp, having adjusted the spectacles to be
ter his eyes, and having thrice thumped h
head upon the floor, he made a carefu
perscrutation of the letter, and from it too
his words:

"*To Hai Pong, Scholar.*

"*Read this, and swiftly obey. I, Sa
Thoong, seated upon the Dragon Throne
my ancestors, desire your opinion upon ce*

tain weighty matters. *Bring your charts and
books of magic. Come upon the back of a
horse."*

Hai Pong trembled—not that he was
frightened, but merely because to tremble
was the custom. Obediently he muttered,
"*Sha shi chien,*" which is fully as good as
"At once, Sir," but really means, "In a short
shower's time." Strictly speaking, then, Hai
Pong was not so obedient as one might think.
For this reason. There *were* no slight
showers—were no clouds—hadn't been for
months. And this was in the summer. And
this was in the bygone days, when heat was
really hot. Seven suns—not six, I say—but
seven—beamed down upon the kingdom.
They were scattered here and there throughout the heavens. Suns were in the north, in
the south, in the east, and one, in another,
the fourth direction. Not a bush in all the
and could cast a shadow. No wind. There
was no breeze—not so much as a capful.
For once the leaves of aspen trees were motionless. The earth was dry as a careful

soldier's powder. And the suns continued to shine. And it was hot. Oh, VERY hot. A torrid day was every day, and the nights were equatorial.

In the morning when the earliest sun was timed to rise, King San Thoong said to his chancellor, "Chancellor, it is hot. The Shen of Winds won't give us a blow. Follow the usual plans this morning. Send eight swift running-men to Nan Shap Village. Have eight more men at Shang Fong Temple. Eight others must stand in harness at Providential Increase Town. Arrange all things as in the past. Only, you might send a few extra men with whips. Dear. Dear. As I have already remarked, it is hot." The chancellor said, "I humbly beg to agree with Your Majesty. (He better had.) Yes. Yes. Hot at the very coolest. If we could put handles on the ponds, why, they'd be tea kettles, already filled and boiling. As to Your Majesty's instructions—I have hired some mountain men. They are swift and surefooted. Will be precisely where the Royal Mouth has ordered."

So, after breakfast the King backed gracefully into his sedan chair. And the bearers placed the poles upon their shoulders. And the men with whips screamed, "Make a breeze. Make a breeze. Get along there, you dilly-dalliers." Swish. Swish. Snap. The whips fell smartly.

It must have been sad for those who were common travelers on the road. Apricot carts were knocked to the ditches. Beggars, in the dust, saw their bowls smashed to pieces. Donkeys took fright and went over the walls. "Get out of the way, you undoubted scamps. The King is riding today." Swish, and snap, and a thrust. All unbelievably modern.

From day-start till drop of night the King would ride. He had a fringed umbrella above his royal head. Only a few of the suns could strike the Mighty Presence. His men were horny-footed, and had no fear of tones. Over the rough and over the smooth, they ran like foxes in a chase. Thus the King idled comfortably in his rushing, man-carried chair, and ever and again he murmured, "What do *I* care if the Shen be unkind? He'll send no wind to cool the earth, but that gives me no worry. I can make a good breeze to whistle through my beard. Man with the whip, have you gone to sleep? The carriers gallop too leisurely on the hills." Swish. Swish. Now go!

At every village were fresh runners to take the sedan poles. If a man fell exhausted between the towns there was always a farmer to be called upon for relief. "Come out of the field, you turnippy fellow. Grasp the pole and carry your King." Swish. "Ha. Now, will you run when I beg you?" The whip-men were chosen for their stout right arms.

Farmers in those days were an independent lot. They were dissatisfied, and highly talkative. They didn't care what they said. So some of them said this, "To what sort of King do we pay taxes? He is no good. Why doesn't he cause the Shen of Winds to cool the earth? He is no good. We are always hot and listless. We faint while hoeing our dolichos. The King is not exercising his authority." Plenty of others re

plied, "Exactly so. We can't thresh our
rice, because there is no wind to blow the
chaff away. The King is too easy-going.
We must have another." And both groups
grumbled in chorus. "The King rides in his
chair by day, and through the night sleeps
coolly in his palace cellar. But we who are
poor farmers have no sedan chairs, and our
cellars hold only toads and poisonous creep-
ers. The King must cause the wind to blow,
to cool the earth and make us glad. If he
doesn't. . . . For *his* sake, we hope he does."

When the riding King heard of these
farmer persons' complainings, he knew that
he faced rebellion. Quite well he realized
that the weather must be changed, and
changed for the better, quickly. Therefore,
he called for his secretary, and dictated a
letter. The letter was addressed to a certain
Wise Man, named Hai Pong. And so, I'm
back where I started—just like the King,
going in a circle.

His Majesty said to Hai Pong, "Hai
Pong, Wise Man, have you books, and charts,
and spectacles, as ordered?" Hai Pong an-

swered, "Yes, Sire, Your Majesty, may your
stature increase. I have them in my hands,
or on my brow, or else upon the donkey's
back. What book, and what page, shall I
read for your pleasure?" The King said,
"I don't know the book. I don't even know
the page. And that is what you must discover. Finger your books, Hai Pong, until
you find directions for raising the wind. Find
a way to persuade the Shen of Winds. The
wind hasn't blown for a sad six months, and
we *must* find a plan for making it come."
Old Hai Pong spoke regretfully, "I am taken
with doubt, Mighty Majesty. Speaking of
books, I might well have left them at home,
and saved them from scuffing when the donkey trotted. I have read the books carefully
from back to front. They hold no instructions for raising the wind." The King bit
his upper lip. That is the gesture of a person who meditates evil. Wisely, Hai Pong
hastened to add, "However, I dare say a
method can be found. But it will have to be
something utterly new. And one can't b

too suspicious of the new." The King interrupted pettishly, "Bother the newness. Toosh. Tush. Proceed, Hai Pong. You have what plan in your mind?"

The Wise Man polished his spectacles to gain time. "Well, Your High and Extremely Mighty Majesty, may you live forever and never have a false adviser. You see, as I understand it, though no doubt I'll express it but vaguely, for I am only an humble beginner in the long, hard study of wisdom, and besides, one of my eyes is weak —often inflamed. . . . (He was trying his best to talk and plan at the same time.) As I say, Your Majesty, Sir, as I, paltry old Hai Pong, understand it, the best, and in fact, the only method is. . . . (The idea came.) This. We must try to coax the Shen of Winds. In this manner. Throughout the kingdom place generous tables under the trees. Appoint men to place, every evening, delectable foods upon the tables. The Shen will discover these foods, and will eat. He will be pleased. He will show his gratitude

by blowing us a wind. You might have a
note on each table, politely requesting a
breeze."

"That is good scheming," said the King.
"I understand completely. Here is a little
bag of gold, Hai Pong."

Tables were placed under trees in every smallest townlet.

Tables were placed under trees in every
smallest townlet, in every almost-a-village.
Royal servants visited every table, every
evening. They set roasted ducks in jelly,
pickled eggs, scallions, shark fins, jujubes,
and cinnamon cakes upon each table. Al-

ways in the morning the tables were bare.
But the Shen was a most ungrateful fellow.
He ate—if eat he did—and never thanked
the King with a breath of breeze. The aspen
trees were as motionless as ever. The days
were given to greater heat. Thermometers
registered anywhere from a hundred to twice
it. Though there were no thermometers then,
and I mention them merely because I thought
of them.

In despair the royal servants piled tables
high with old ham and new chicken.

This period is known in History as The
Year of Fat Beggars.

The farmers talked louder, and were seen
to sharpen their scythes. Hai Pong received
another letter from the King.

"To Hai Pong:

*Read and run. I, San Thoong, in the
Dragon Chair, desire to hear your head
thump upon the Presence Room floor. Bring
the little bag of gold with you. I didn't rest
at all comfortably last night. Come upon
the back of a horse."*

Hai Pong owned no horse. He had only a donkey in the shape of a horse. The sad and dim-eyed Wise Man tucked the bag of

This year is known in History as: the year of fat beggars.

gold under his girdle. He placed his little daughter, Fan Shih Chu, upon the fore of the saddle, and said to the donkey, "Get along. But not so very fast. I wish to hear the birds at their singing." He took his daughter with him, for it was common knowledge that the King's dudgeon was oftenest made known by a sweep of the sword-arm. He wished to leave Fan Shih Chu with an aunt in Chang An City. The aunt would see to Fan Shih's future, and comfort her in respect to her father's untimely taking to the Land of The Long Dark Shadows.

The world was brown and dry that morning. But the world was very beautiful. Hai Pong sorrowed as he mused. "So beautiful. And so soon I must leave it forever. Riding swiftly to my grave. Steady, donkey. Steady."

In the Presence Chamber. The King passioned his voice. Hai Pong industriously bumped the floor with his forehead. The headsman, evil fellow, with much suggestive noise, rubbed a whetstone upon the edge of his sabre. The look of things was bad. "Is there any reason at all why you should continue in life? No." His Majesty beckoned to the headsman.

Fortunately, the chancellor entered with

some extremely fine plums, sent by special
caravan from the Yellow Lama's Land.
Good for the chancellor. The plums had
golden pits.

After a while the King remarked. "Now,
Hai Pong, I have pardoned you for the last
time. Use your life well. The Shen still
sulks and will give no breeze. Think of a
plan to persuade the Shen to do his duty."
Hai Pong had a scheme ready for his tongue.
"Sire, The King, in our first attempt we used
the best of kindness to the Shen. Nothing
is kinder than meat and cakes. But the Shen
was scornful. He thought us weak. So, it
behooves us to throw the Shen in fright. We
must prove to him he is not master. Make
him tremble. Make him weep. You, Most
Mild Majesty, have firecrackers, rockets, pin-
wheels, and other astounding powder devices
in your treasury. Fire these instruments into
the sky—for a week, perhaps. I make no
doubt the Shen will be so frightened he will
gladly send us a wind to cool the earth.'
The King said, "Your plan is based on common sense. Fear is a mighty mover. Take

this little bag of gold, Hai Pong. Chancellor, search out the treasurer—he's somewhere playing fan tan, and have the vaults unlocked."

The King ordered all of his porters into the treasury to carry out bales of fireworks. Throughout the city, punk fires glowed, and the people lighted crackers. Pop. . . . Poppytypop. . . . Ker-pow. Firecrackers rifted the lower air. The rockets, more ambitious, ripped the heavens. Pop. . . . Pop. . . . Popping everywhere. That was another good thing they had in Kiang Sing—good powder. The King was as ardent in firing as any soldier's son. The little girl, Fan Shih, did her part with the best of men. She lighted the reddest firecrackers and tossed them skyward. And one tremendous firepiece of her tossing struck the King's high flagstaff, and was deflected to a portico pillar, and from there it fell to the chancellor's head (no harm done, yet), and from the chancellor's head it bounced into the thick of King San Thoong's beard. And there it acted as a conscientious cracker should. It burnt all the middle from

King San's beard. And much talk was heard. "What villain threw it, do you think?" "I saw an old man wearing a peculiar hat." "This means work for the headsman."

But when the King recovered from the shock, he felt rather well pleased. His beard was forked in a way he thought beautiful. In fact, the forked beard has been popular ever since.

Hai Pong and Fan Shih Chu rode home on their donkey. The little girl was frightened. Hai Pong was sad and uncertain. The poor man began to doubt if his plan for Shen-scaring would succeed. Often he raised a finger hoping to feel a stir of wind. But the air was as still as a porcelain mouse in a well-behaved zoölogical park.

The Wise Man didn't linger very long in his dwelling. He rolled many books, some clothing, plenty of rice, and three assorted dolls in a tent cloth. With the budget on his back, he went to the kitchen door and called loudly for Fan Shih. "COME TO SUP-PER, FAN SHIH. COME. COME. YOU ANI THE CAT." That was to deceive the neighbors, in case they might be listening, which, of course, they were. Fan Shih said, "Why do you shout so, Daddy? Here I am, right at your side." "Kuar. Kuar ti, child," (Hush. Hush) whispered Hai Pong. "Softly. Speak softly, Daughter. You and I must go far from here. The King will be angry if firecrackers fail. He will surely separate me—breath forever from the body. Let us go to a cave I know in the hills. There we can hide and be safe of head." Fan Shih Chu said, "I am very fond of caves. Though I hope no toads are there. Is it a big cave, Daddy? Are you afraid of toads?" Her anxious father whispered, "Kuar. Kuar ti. Sssssh. We must talk softly as dream-cats on a carpet." Through the night and into the morning, they hastened by unfrequented paths to the hills.

For several days the two kept hidden in their cave. Hai Pong suffered intensely. Not from heat. Not from lack of food. But, because he couldn't read. The cavern was too dark. So Hai Pong set his mind upon thinking, and by and by was inspired with a plan. But the plan depended upon Fan Shih's aid. The Wise Man explained to his daughter, "Child, your poor old father can't live another hour unless he strengthens himself with books. And you must help him. While he reads in the light outside our door, Fan Shih must watch from yonder hill. If Fan Shih sees men riding in the distance, she must scream. Whereupon her father will quickly drop back into the cavern. Do you understand?"

"I know it perfectly," answered Fan Shih. "And I'm glad you'll let me go to the flowers and the sunlight. I've been getting weary of nothing but dolls and darkness."

Hai Pong sat in the light and read. His little daughter perched upon a hill top.

No persons with swords could be seen. Presently, Fan Shih decided to gather flowers. A tiny, timid rabbit hopped out from a bush. Fan Shih thought him a toad, or possibly, a dragon. She wasn't sure. But that made no difference.

Hai Pong read aloud from his book. "H

who hurries cannot walk with a stately step."
It's a proverb.

Fan Shih's voice came to him clearly.
"Oh-h-h-h-h-hh."

Hai Pong read no more. The Wise Man
hurled his book into the cavern. An instant
later he had hurled himself after it. His
step, be well assured, was nothing stately.
For, as the proverb has it, "He who hurries
cannot walk with a stately step." There was
much grieving over broken spectacles.

Next day Hai Pong instructed his daughter further. "I fear you may see another
rabbit—and—such haste is not good for my
bones. If you see army persons coming, do
this, my child—scream first, then flourish
your hat. By the hat I shall know the
danger."

Upon the hill top, Fan Shih gazed a while,
then played a while. Presently it was time
to gaze again. Afar, toward the capital city,
were men who glittered in the sunshine.
Spearmen. . . . Soldiers. . . . "Oh-h-h-h-h-
h-hh." Fan Shih frantically waved her hat.

She felt a sudden breeze. The daughter of Hai Pong continued to wave. She felt a breeze each time. So the child thought, at first, the danger was over—the Shen had sent a wind.

But when Fan Shih stopped waving, the breezes also stopped. Nevertheless, she hastened to the cave to tell her father what had happened.

Old Hai Pong was dumfounded. He waved the hat at himself many times. "It isn't explained in the books, Daughter, but undoubtedly it is true. We must both thank you for this invention. It has saved our lives, I know, for my head once more feels my very own." The Wise Man put his mind to work. He fastened Fan Shih's hat to a stick. That was his first improvement—gave the hat a handle. Half the night he sat awake, making breezes in the cave, thinking of other betterments.

On the road to Chang An City, Hai Pong and his daughter met soldiers. "Don't move. Stand where you are till we chain you." The captain's voice was harsh as that of a general

Fan Shih hastened to tell her father what had happened.

"Unceasingly we have searched for you, Hai Pong. By the use of fine sagacity we have found you. Come with us to the King and the sword." The Wise Man said, "I am now on my way to the palace." He flourished Fan Shih's hat in the captain's face. The captain felt a breeze, and stepped back thirty paces. His men-at-arms shamelessly ran. They knew that Hai Pong had a reputation for magic. But the captain, who had run his thirty paces, scolded the spearmen for being not brave . . . they had run a hundred.

King San Thoong rubbed his plump hands gleefully. "Ah. The man who frightens the Shen has come. Have you any excuse at all, Hai Pong? The wind is as absent as ever. Have you any remotest, unlikely excuse? Just a moment, headsman. Let him speak." Hai Pong said boldly, "No excuse, Your Majesty, but I have a small, successful maker of breezes." He waved Fan Shih's hat in the King's moist face. Back went His Majesty, out of the chair.

"It blows. It blows. It's the wind on a stick."

The King soon put his artisans to making
Fan Shih hats. He exalted some of his page
boys to a newly created rank—"Waver-of-

He waved Fan Shih's hat.

Fan-Shih-hat." Heat no longer disturbed
him. He rode no more the whole day
through. In the palace he took his leisure
amid breezes. His handicraftsmen improved

the Fan Shih hat. They lowered its crown
and made it all in a level piece. Thus by
degrees, they perfected that instrument of
cooling which we of today call a "Fan."

This will be a trifle concerning the Shen.
The sulky fellow soon learned of the Fan
Shih hat. He was extremely angry. He
thought the King had gone a step too far.
In his especial rage he brought a big wind to
the city.

One thousand ounces of silver it cost to
put a new roof on the palace.

KINGS HUNGRY

AH YAY was not one of the kings. He
was a boy person, about so old, and merely
so tall, more or less. He lived with his
uncle, Chum Kuey, in a house rather small,
near the hard bottomed road to Chang An
City. Ah Yay, I have heard, was a fairly
good boy, as boys went in those long past
days. In fact he was quite kind-hearted,

both to man and beast. He never threw stones at tigers, and never cried "Boo" at the military brave-men marching. Now and then, it may be true, he forgot to gather the red hen's eggs of an evening, but he always roasted potatoes to the right degree of crumbliness, and he boiled water for the tea most admirably.

And, there's no complaint to be made of Uncle Chum Kuey. He was a miller. His coat was white, but his cat was black. If his cat was black, then, of course, he *had* a cat, but he had no wife in the house—he was not married. Neither was Ah Yay married, at least, not likely. Except for their cat, the two had a house pretty much to themselves.

Ah Yay's duty it was to do his best in the kitchen, to cook the food and see that the kitchen idol's lips were always coated with honey. But when any especial holiday came near, then Uncle Kuey took in his hand the willow wood ladle. Hence, when the Feast of Lanterns was soon to be, Uncle Kuey attended to the baking. The house was filled with coaxing odors. Firstly, were cake

called melt-in-the-mouth. Secondly, dumplings rich with preserved pumpkin blossoms.
Thirdly, shark fins. Cabbages heaped in a
largest pot. Carambolas between sheets of
dough. Apples that had ripened into red,
hidden under coats of sugar gum. Old eggs
out of the ashes. Arbutus fruit in red sugar.
But choicest of all was a fat pig's ham.
Upon the ham Uncle Kuey had spent his best
efforts. "Fit for the king, may he live forever." So spoke Uncle Kuey, and not a word
that wasn't justified. "They have fine dishes
in the palace, but I respectfully doubt if a
better ham ever went to His Majesty's table.
And by the way, Ah Yay, speaking of His
Majesty reminds me. If the king should
come to our house, don't be alarmed. There's
been much thieving in high places. I pay
tax on every grist I grind in the mill, but
the tax money seldom goes through the door
of His Majesty's treasury. There's a tale
that the king is making secret inspections to
discover why he is poor, and the people are
poor, while mandarins grow wealthy." Ah
Yay said, "If the king comes I'll dust off our

best black-wood chair and ask His Majesty
to sit, while I run to the mill with news.
Will that be right to do?" His uncle replied, "Right, and quickly thought of, but,
my oh my, I'm letting our golden lily cakes
go to black cinders." And so he was, and the
pity of it.

Feast days always seem to tarry. Musing
of pleasant foods, Ah Yay sat under a bo
tree and waited for tomorrow to come. In
stead of tomorrow, a dusty old man came up
from the road. He was slow-walking, bent
unkempt in a word, and a very popular word
with story-tellers. The greybeard gazed a
Ah Yay with great deliberation. Ah Yay
didn't know the old fellow, nevertheless he
felt impelled to speak. He decided upon
number three of the recommended greetings
"I congratulate you, Great Man, on having
acquired bountiful wealth." (And the visitor
in tatters.) The old man responded, "You
are a polite boy, not like others, who speak
ill-chosen words, and throw clods. You will
rise in the world, and be the king's trues
man." And then, as if a surprising idea had

popped into his mind, he exclaimed, "The king, may he catch all mandarin thieves. Young man under the bo tree, have you ever seen the king?" Ah Yay shook his head. "No, not once. I have seen his sedan chair pass, but the curtains were always drawn close." Visitor greybeard laughed shrewdly, "Your king doesn't always travel in rolling chariot and carried chair. He foots it too. Often he dresses in poor clothing and mingles with the people. He gowns in cloth no better than mine, and goes forth to see what a beggar may see." A strong suspicion arose in Ah Yay's mind. He inquired, somewhat shakily, "Are you really His Majesty, The King?" The bearded one was prompt in denying all relationship to royalty, but only in a half-hearted way, not with any show of anger. "Oh, really, you know, you must not call me His Majesty—though I must admit I am familiar with the palace halls. By the way, have you any food in the undoubtedly clean-kept kitchen? A change of food might start my appetite." The way he carried his beard made Ah Yay quite positive. Only a king

could be so high-chinned. Only a king could
be so bearded.

"Oh, yes, Your Merciful Majesty." The
words were stammered. "We have much
food of the kind we humble people eat.
There are sweet cakes spiced, and cabbage,
pig's meat and more. Rice I'll put in the
kettle at once. Then, while you sit high in
our best black-wood chair, I'll go to summon
my uncle from the mill." "Never mind,"
said the guest. "Don't bother. I have much
to see this afternoon, and cannot linger. My
feet are soon for the road. I'll take some
cakes and pickled eggs, and ah, how lucky
yes . . . the ham." He put these things in
his straw beggar's-wallet, and having given
thanks, with spectacular strut he entered the
road.

Uncle Chum Kuey, at home late from
work, looked high and low for the ham. He
might have wasted candles all night if he
hadn't thought to question Ah Yay, in the
quilts. He awoke the sleeping boy. "Did
you, Ah Yay, or our cat, get the pig's ham?
If neither one, then what has become of it?"

Ah Yay knew where the meat had gone. He
was willing and eager to talk. Oh, so
proudly he informed Uncle Kuey. "Just as
you said the king might do, he came to our
house this morning. I recognized him by
his royal beard. He was very hungry, but
wouldn't sit. Graciously he accepted the
ham, and said he'd remember our house with
favor." "He should," said Uncle Kuey. "I
fear your guest was far less than a king.
The king wears mustaches, not a beard. The
taker of our ham, no doubt, is only a wanderer man who has heard of the king's habit
to go among the people. Don't let him deceive you again. Should the real king come
to our garden gate, by all means give him
delicate food. But beware of the want-rice-
men (the beggars). Give them rice alone,
and spare our costly ham."

Men went up the Chang An road, and men
went down. One of them stopped to open
the gate, to enter the gate and ask, "Is this
the house of Wang Po Lu?" He was a
straight-standing man with an air of im-
portance. His face was mustached and stern.

He had the air of a Ning Pan stormy dragon. Ah Yay greeted him with respectful bows. "May you eat red rice as long as you live, and

He was a straight-standing man with an air of importanc

go to your grave in a nan wood coffin. (An that's wishing good luck, here and hereafter No, this isn't the house of Wang Po L and I never heard of him. My uncle, Chum Kuey, is owner of this house, and the garden, and the mill, and in the mill is where he's now at work."

The straight man smiled. "Oh, yes. Chum Kuey, the large tax-payer. He has good qualities, and I hope will come into a fortune. If he were here I know he would recognize me, and ask me to dine upon delicate foods." Ah Yay immediately began to wonder. Indubitably the man had an uncommon mustache, and the strength, and the voice. Could he be? Why not query him? "How is it you know of my uncle, and taxes? Are you the king?" The stranger went into a frown. "One must always be guarded in speech if a secret is to be kept. However, there's little of harm in admitting I am not unknown in the palace." That made it quite plain to Ah Yay. He had a king for company. In his best inviting manner he said, "If it won't harm your boots to tread our worthless garden, please will Your Majesty come in? We have common food, but set out in plenty. Sit upon our finest black-wood chair to dine, while I go summon my uncle." "Oh, never mind that," said the hungry man. "I haven't the time to wait. What are these? Old eggs?" They were. Eggs six months bettered in lime. They were black of the white, and green of yolk, perfectly delightful. The happy king (at least he hadn't said he wasn't) filled a straw beggar's-wallet. And "Good boy I call you," said he. And "Thanks everlasting," he said. "Say to your honorable uncle I shall hold him pleasantly in memory." He stepped off toward Chang An, city of riches and splendor

When Uncle Chum Kuey came home in the night, he was hungry. With a hungry man it's a most natural thing to think of pickled eggs. Uncle Kuey did so. He looked here and there, and in the other place. Not even a shell he found. He might have searched till the sad, sure day of doom if he hadn't thought to waken and question his nephew. Information soon came from the bed quilts. "The eggs? Oh, yes, Uncle Kuey. The king came with his girdle drawn tight. He was hungry through and through, Uncl

Kuey. But he wouldn't sit, and he couldn't wait. He graciously took the eggs, and thanked us much. Being very large, he took a great many eggs."

Uncle Kuey said, "You were deceived, Ah Yay. The tall man is only a beggar chief. I have seen him, but I shall never more see my eggs. Don't be imposed upon again. The king is a little man. Should our one and only king come hungry, be sure to feed him. Delicate food for the king, but plain, small rice for beggars, only make sure they don't take the kettle also. And use your wits another time; don't believe more than you hear."

Ah Yay was still expecting the king. Every journeyer that used the road was well stared at and measured. The proudest man to stop at the gate was a donkey driver, but even he proved somewhat disappointing. He wanted only a drink. Ah Yay asked him, 'Are you His Majesty, looking for taxes?" The driver said, "No. I'm a lover of peace and the head on my shoulders. Therefore, rule over donkeys, not men."

At last, with slow hobbling, came another stranger to the house. This person was a shatterer of hope. Ah Yay sat him down at once as being no king. The man had a droop to his mouth, and a sadness behind his eyes. He had a stoop in his spine, and his mustache was ten hairs to each side. As mild looking person as ever tinkered pans. For all that, Ah Yay was not one to let go of politeness. He used the second usual greeting. "I hope you have lately eaten rice." The old man chirped, "Yes, thank you. I saw the bottom of the bowl," that being the customary answer. Even a starving man is supposed to answer, "Thank you, yes," unless, perchance, he wishes to be thought a boor, or drunk and below good manners. "I rejoice," said Ah Yay, "and hope you may live several thousand years longer." The strange little fellow mourned, "Thank you again, but I fear I shan't live an hour longer unless some kind kitchen-person gives me a flitch of bacon, or a side of fish."

Ah Yay had expected a remark of the kind "Ko lien, (what a pity) but we have n bacon, no fish, no shoulder, no ham, not even a bone." "None of those things? Then eggs. Have you got 'em? Have you got any eggs with an age to them?" Ah Yay saw through the old fellow's scheme at once. He wanted eggs. The boy was determined not to be bamboozled. "No," he said, "No eggs today. All I can give you is rice and well-water. Sit here in shade while I do the dishing." The stranger murmured dolorously, "I'd rather have some bear's flesh. I'd rather have torpedo roe. But it seems my rathers must go ungranted." He sat down on a stone and Ah Yay soon gave him a smoking bowl.

The ancient and true saying is "A gift of hot rice warms hands and heart." Ah Yay's gift of rice was exceedingly hot; it warmed hands and heart like a fever. The old man gasped and exclaimed, "Give me water." But instead of waiting to be given a drink, he grasped the draw-rope, and promptly tumbled down the well. He made the sound of a frog at the bottom, then screamed incoherently of ropes, and a chancellor.

Ah Yay was quite strong for his size. The unfortunate stranger, fortunately, was light. The rope was of a best sort. At one end of the rope clung the old man, guggling. At the upper end Ah Yay pulled with his utmost power. Just as he thought he could pull no more, he saw a wet hand raised to grasp the well curb.

The aged stranger shook himself, then sat down and calmly finished his rice. But Ah Yah was more tired than he had ever been in all his days before. He stretched him out in the shade of the bo tree, and there he lay a long time, feeling weak and utterly without ambition. It was the pleasantest time of summer, with flowers in blossom, and bees bumbling, and grass like a mandarin's green carpet. The little wind-bells tinkled from the house eaves. A drowsily restful day.

All too soon for Ah Yay the afternoon passed and Uncle Chum Kuey returned from work. The uncle was much excited. "What mischief have you been up to?" Ah Yay had a fairly serene conscience. "Why, nothing worse than usual, Uncle Kuey. I gave

Just as he thought he could pull no more, he saw a wet hand.

an old want-rice-man food. . . ." Uncle
Kuey stopped him. "I fear something terrible is about to happen. A royal sedan chair
waits down the road, and a large and important king's servant demands of all passers
by if they know in what house lives Ah
Yay. I fear. I fear. Perhaps you'd better
hide."

Ah Yay, too, was inclined to tremble a bit.
Nevertheless, he spoke spiritedly enough. "I
don't imagine there's any cause for shaking.
More than likely the man wants another person named Ah Yay."

But Ah Yay was mistaken. The important man in royal livery questioned him.
"Are you the Ah Yay who pulled the rope?
Hao. His Majesty demands your presence
at once. Please enter the chair." Ah Yay
stumbled under the curtains, and felt himself
lifted. Then the carriers shouted, and feet
pattered, and travelers climbed to the side
of the road and gabbled. "Royalty is passing." Ah Yay heard them, and liked himself
much better. It was a new experience to be
called "Royalty."

It was another new experience to enter the palace. Ah Yay found himself within the throne room, on his knees, knocking his head upon the marble pave. After a time he realized that the king was speaking. Evidently His Majesty had been speaking for some while. "And so, I trust that I am not lacking in appreciation. I appoint you a page in the royal household. Be faithful in all things. Arise, Ah Yay. Chamberlain, see that he receives proper clothing. Treasurer, I learned the names of two more mandarins who consistently defraud us. Write as I speak. . . ."

When the haze of surprise finally cleared from Ah Yay's mind, he ceased to fumble with his purple silken gown, for he knew it was real, and his new life was real. For duty, he had to wait upon the king, find his spectacles, and fan him, and be quick to tell the cook, "More tea." He thought the king much finer looking in robes of state than in the disguise attire worn that stirring day in the well. His Majesty's mustache still needed more of it; however, it was probably fairly good average mustache.

The king had an immense garden; miles
to its farthest wall. In the royal garden
were all known flowers and trees. Brooks
and fishes, hills and spotted deer, these
things. Cockatoos, and pretty apes, and lusty
voiced peafowl, those things. A royal garden, and that describes it. Every evening
the king walked in his garden to breathe the
fresh, reviving air. Ah Yay always went
along, to carry fans, and kerchiefs, and
wanted snuff boxes. Usually he kept his eyes
alert to see the gaudy peafowl, and so it
chanced that he saw a man creep out of a
flowered bush and steal upon the king. This
man had an evil glare in his eyes, evidently
fanatic.

Ah Yay had no weapon in his girdle.
With only his strength to rely on, he sprang
between the intruder and the king. "Go
away at once," he commanded. "His Majesty will be displeased if you do not leave.
This is the royal garden, and trespassers are
forbidden." The answer came in a stroke
upon his breast. His Majesty's valiant page

staggered, but struck back. Another terrific blow fell upon him. The royal garden vanished.

When Ah Yay opened his eyes, Uncle Chum Kuey was stooped above him, tapping gently. "Wake up. Wake up, sleepy-head. The sun is gone, and the owls are out."

It's a great come down from being His Majesty's purple clothed page, to being merely a boy in a mere man's garden. On the other hand, it's decidedly more pleasant to be safe under a bo tree, than slain under oleanders. Ah Yay felt distinctly glad to be living. He rubbed his eyes, and murmured, "Only a *dream*. Dear me, I have been asleep and dreaming. Such an exciting dream, Uncle Kuey. I must hurry, and get your supper at once."

His uncle said, "You'll have more things than supper to think of. I fear some trouble is upon us. Have you unwittingly disturbed the peace of the realm today?"

"No, indeed, Uncle Kuey. I gave a man some little rice, and he tumbled down the well, but I pulled him out, and nothing was broken. Why do you look so alarmed?"

"Because," said his uncle, "there's a royal sedan chair in the road, and a consequentially dressed man is asking all who pass if they know where lives Ah Yay."

WING DOW

They've raised a monument to Wing Dow. It's a pai lou, of one high and two low arches, standing on the Monkey Hill, down in Kiang Sing. But I don't see why they built it. Wing Dow was a scamp. If e wasn't a scamp, why did he come to Chang wan's house in the thick of night? Why id he try to make off with Chang Jwan's pretty daughter? Is it proper to steal an honest farmer's daughter?

Wing Dow straightened up to stand in his master's potato field. "A tremendous heat has fallen upon us, honorable Chang Jwan. My fan does me no cooling whatsoever. And my throat's as dry as the kiang kou jin's oldest story." (That was a dig at the story-teller.) The lazy fellow's remarks had merely a casual sound. No one would have suspected that he contemplated a trick. Chang Jwan continued to place his hand upon potatoes. "Yes, *industrious* Wing Dow," said Chang Jwan. (But surely he didn't mean it.) "There is much heat in the field, and truth in what you say. Indeed yes." Steadily he flung potatoes into the basket; fanning with one hand, and farming with the other.

"I fear you are beginning to thirst for what's in the well, honorable Chang Jwan. Shall I not fetch water?" He set his feet in the direction he wished to travel. Chang Jwan, far from having suspicion, felt pleased that Wing should be so thoughtful. "I am rather the worse for lack of drink. Certainly you may go. My daughter, Seeah See See, was to bring us a bucketful, but, no doubt, she has forgotten, or is busy at the loom."

But Seeah See See had not forgotten. And she wasn't weaving. There she was in plain sight, on her way to the well; had the bucket, had the gourd. But the old one, grey Chang Jwan, didn't see his daughter. His eyes were only for potatoes. Wing Dow was the one who saw. He went away whistling, hopping furrows blithely, thinking of pretty words to speak.

Wing Dow was a trifle tied-of-tongue at first. He had rehearsed the poetic "Your eyes are like the two bright lakes in Kwen Lun Shan, where fairy barges voyage forth with all delights the world will ever know." But to save him he couldn't say it. He gave up poesy for the practical. "Let me fill the bucket, Seeah See See. Really, you shouldn't lean over the well. Dangerous, snapping frogs are in it. Were you to fall—Oh, dear! Let my rough, eager hand uphaul the bucket." Seeah See See said, "Thank you, Wing Dow."

Let me fill the bucket, Seeah See See.

The young man meditated a short while, and out of his meditation came remembrance. "Your eyes are like the two bright lakes. . . ." And so forth. And so forth. Seeah See See smiled.

Other words, rhythmic and wilder, rushed to Wing Dow's mind, and he spoke them fervently—this, and that, and your voice so like a silver bell. No one would believe the many things he said, so there isn't any good to be had by repetition.

After so long while the two at the well took thought of a potato field, and a thirsty man within it. They went—Wing Dow with the bucket, and Seeah See See with the calabash. Old Chang Jwan was glad to see them come. He smiled—but that was before he dipped the gourd. The imposed-upon farmer squinted at the bucket. He frowned severely. "How is this, Wing Dow? You were to bring water. Yet, you fetch a bucket brimfilled with emptiness—and nothing else—not even a frog in it—though I don't want one. How is this, Wing Dow? Is the water well dry?"

Wing Dow had forgotten to get what he went for. He hadn't even touched the water with his bucket. Hadn't dropped the bucket even half way down. But he escaped punishment. Luckily he thought of an excuse, something like, "Dear me in trouble. The bucket surely leaks. How bad of it. Dear. Dear. We'll have to go again." Chang Jwan glared at him. Terribly hot, it was in the field. A great wonder the farmer didn't rise to an unkindness. He was a man of scant patience; large-handed, and thewed of arm.

Wing Dow paid three cash to a strolling scholar for a little book of poems. I can't say what the name was, but it was a red-bound book. Wing Dow memorized all the poems, and of nights would sing them to the moon—as if the moon cared. Though perhaps it did. But, yes or no, as you please for the moon, it is certain that some of the villagers cared. They said that Wing Dow's singing alarmed them from slumber, and made affidavit of this trouble to the mayor Chang Jwan's care was for another cause

He complained that Wing Dow was not worth his pepper (let alone salt) in the field of ripe potatoes: that he flung indifferent clods in the basket, and left the valuable "earth-eggs" ungathered in the furrow. The farmer declared he would be compelled to hire a man not blind, to help in the field of harvest.

To tell of Seeah See See is to praise. She was a maid that took the eye. And more than prettiness she had. To use little ink in description, old daddy Chang Jwan's house was neatest in the whole village. Seeah See See went about her daily tasks light-heartedly, but with thoroughtude. Not once did she place the rice kettle out of doors, and the cat upon the stove. (But they say Wing Dow, the wit-wandering fellow, did precisely that.) Seeah See See embroidered silken chrysanthemums, made cinnamon dumplings, took plums from the tree, and did all other things, with a hand as neat as it was here-and-there and busy at something else. For her father she wove a blue stuff coat, and even the neighbors admitted that the coat was perfect in looming and fit—though they thought the color a bit off, and said as much.

But it's time to get down to potatoes. Had Wing Dow held such a thought perhaps he'd have heard more pleasant speaking. Chang Jwan had been bearishly cross in the field. He had spoken harshly, yes, derisively of Wing Dow's lack of eyes, and undoubtedly moon-struck appearance. And Wing Dow was hot from the sun, and hotter with indignation. He felt a desire to chuck Chang Jwan with the largest potato in reach, and trust to his heels for the haste that would be needed. But he didn't. He tossed the "earth-egg" into the basket, and quaveringly spoke to the master-of-the-field. "Honorable Excellent Farmer, I am a person of little account. . . ."

"Oh, *don't* say that," exclaimed Chang Jwan, so sweetly that his meaning was quite plain.

"It is true. Quite worthless. I should have the bamboo for daring to ask, yet, ask I do, for your. . . ."

"Bamboo? You shall have it, in the

twinkling of a bedpost. Gather potatoes, you very-little-worker. Are you a story-teller, paid to babble?"

The savage tone of it caused Wing Dow to bend. Pretending to be at work, he continued to ask, for whatever it may have been. "Honorable Farmer, please be more forbearing. I wish to ask you for your. . . ." Chang Jwan made no reply. He merely roared. A roar without words. And the trees at the field edge trembled, and Wing Dow fell over his basket, and righted it, and in went potatoes as fast as they could. That farmer was honest enough, and worthy, but there are no good words for his roar.

The day that came next was the worse for too much sun. The field was lively with quiver heat. At the hour called yang, which is hottest, Wing Dow found excuse for a jaunt to the well. Of course, he hadn't expected to find Seeah See See at the well. Of course not. But there she was; her cheeks ivory-pink, and her hair in the butterfly manner. Wing and the maiden talked rather excitedly, but every word a whisper nonetheless, until the very end. When Wing Dow started back to the field he said, "Tonight. I'll come with the donkey, sharply on the hour." Seeah See See cautioned him, "But don't touch the southern wall. Use care. Oh, use the stillest care."

In Kiang Sing every house has its door set in the southern wall. That is the custom; and there's good reason—and a long explanation for it. The farmer, Chang Jwan, always slept close to his door—and had good reason for it. He was a man of silver wealth, supposedly buried under the floor. Should thieves chance to pry at his door, their work would likely (would certainly) rouse the vigilant householder. His bed touched the door, and his hand touched a scythe throughout the hours of sleep.

By light of a half-made moon came Wing Dow, creeping, to the northern wall of Chang Jwan's house. With an iron bar, feloniously used, he tore bricks from the wall. In a little while he forced an opening through which a cat might have crawled. Wing was jubilant. Tied to a nearby tree was his donkey,

facing the Tumbled Mountains, ready to
trot. Clothing and kettles were roped to the
saddle. . . . And old Chang Jwan asleep.

Mortar flew. The bricks came loose. Poor
old Chang Jwan. . . . How sad he would be
in the morning. Very, very sad. His daughter would be far away—and happy—in a

Oh, you low-thoughted thief.

hidden cottage in the Tumbled Mountains.
Wing Dow worked with quicker strokes.
Down fell another brick. Upon it fell Wing
Dow. Upon Wing Dow descended a wild
and weighty something that kicked, and
cuffed, and screamed horribly to hear. "Oh,
you low-thoughted thief." A few more
thumpings. "Oh, you rapscallion." A

pause in his speech while he drove down
blows. "Villainous breaker-in. . . . What?
What's that you say??? You are Wing
Dow?????" The one underneath was
pleading, "Forgive me, Honorable Chang
Jwan. It was done in a dream. I came in
deep slumber, dreaming. I thought the
bricks were potatoes, in my dream, and so,
I dug. . . . All for you, Chang Jwan,—working for you." The farmer arose. "If that
be true, then I have wronged you with my
strikings. Forgive me, Wing Dow. Why,
here is your donkey, saddled and packed.
That's queer. You should see the doctor.
Get medicines, Wing Dow, to moderate your
dreams." The strong farmer returned to his
bed, somewhat worried, and somewhat mysti-
fied. Wing Dow, looking like a man who
had fallen in mouths of wolves, limped off
to the village.

Doctor Chen Twom had a reputation old
and unassailable. When he said, "This patient will live," the mourners always retired,
baffled, to their houses, for they knew there'd
be no grave to dig. The doctor had a hun-

dred medicines, and could cure as many troubles. When he saw Wing Dow approaching, he at once took bamboo tubes from his cabinet. "You came just in time, young fellow my lad. Shih huey, that's for your broken bruises. Grated chan pu for contusions. Chiang yao for the splintered bones. . . ." Wing Dow interposed, "No. No. Doctor. I came, not because of these hurts you *see*. I came for other aid. I . . . I. . . . Doctor, I am love-stricken."

The old physician selected a dozen tubes. "The cost will be rather high. But—I can cure it." "No. No. Doctor. No cure I want. I want Seeah See See. But we can't elope without waking her honorable father. And—he strikes unmercifully. You, Doctor, have sleeping pow. . . ." The doctor rolled his eyes. "Unless Chang Jwan really needs them, it would be unethical to give him the powders for compelled-sleep. You must think of another plan, Wing Dow. I am your friend, and will help you—but not unthically."

Wing Dow was unaccustomed to compli-

cated thinking. He made a ferocious face,
and heady, squeaking noises. We who are
habited to the deep, long thoughts can hardly
imagine the strain poor Wing Dow felt. His
mind ran thus: "My contusions pain me.
Honorable Chang Jwan caused them. His
anger was intense—merely because I came
to his house by night, and made an opening
in his northern wall. Opening in the wall.
Opening." He whooped for gladness. "I
have it, Doctor. Can you prepare a medicine
that will cause Chang Jwan to forget the
opening in his wall—or, better, will cause
him to enlarge it?"

"I have medicines for all purposes—and
no purpose at all—though that's a profes-
sional secret." Proudly. "I can make Chang
Jwan climb a tree, or stand on his head, or
whatever I please."

Wing made sounds of pleasure. "Then
congratulate me, Doctor. And—here is your
fee." After a trifle more of heads-together
scheming, the two said, "Hao."

Doctor Chen Twom began to tear a hole
in the north wall of his office. Wing Dow

went home and tore a hole in the north wall
of his kitchen.

The disturbance of the night had done ill
for Chang Jwan. The farmer was pale. His
daughter, Seeah See See, opened her eyes
wide. "Dear. Dear. What is wrong, Honorable Daddy? You are so white—so pale
—and you tremble. Hadn't you better visit
Doctor Chen Twom?" The father replied,
"Nonsense. I feel lightsome, chirpy, too—
jolly as a sparrow in springtime." But Seeah
See See sighed dolorously, and set bitters on
the table.

Wing Dow was the scamp. Trust Wing
Dow to spare no exaggeration. "Dear, and
double dear, Honorable Chang Jwan. Surely
you are ill. Why, you're the likest to a ghost
I ever saw. Your face is whiter than powdered rice. If you live till time for supper,
I'll be greatly surprised." "What nonsense
is this?" exclaimed the farmer, angrily. "I
feel tolerably well. Not overly ailing.
Gather potatoes, Wing Dow. Think of them,
and not my disabilities."

Wing Dow filled baskets, but every now

and then he murmured, with sufficient loud-
ness, "Dear. Dear. So white. So ill."
After a time, the farmer said, "I'll be going
now. Kindly continue to gather potatoes,
Wing Dow. I shall be back shortly—unless
ordered to do otherwise." Off he went toward the village. The man was altogether
in health. Yet, his head drooped. He
dragged a foot. He groaned. Simply
couldn't help it.

In the potato field, Wing Dow moaned
louder and louder, until he shouted, "So
white. So ill." "So ill. So white," while
his master was in hearing. Then Wing's
pretended sadness dropped from him, and he
sang like any gleeman at a fair.

Doctor Chen Twom had always been noted
for his calmness, even when confronted by
most terrifying sights. But now, he chose to
be greatly agitated. "Are you a flesh-man
or a ghost-man? Oh, you are still yourself.
You are still Chang Jwan? Good gracious."
He began to take medicine tubes, four at a
time, from the cabinet. As solemnly as a
hanging judge, he again spoke to his shake

patient. "My dear sir, my very dear sir, you came no sooner than you should. Bad. Bad." He was examining the medicine tubes. "Merciful me. I have no hui ku yao. . . . Let me study the rules. . . . I've got to go deep in the book for this case. . . . Humph. . . . Dark in the house. The house is too dark." Most ostentatiously he carried his book to the newly made hole-in-the-wall. There he read it very well. "Air. Air. Air. That's the complete cure, Chang Jwan. You need fresh air."

"Goodness alive, Doctor, I'm *in* the fresh air from far before the sun comes up, until the owls have flown an hour."

Doctor Chen Twom could put much austerity in his voice. "Tush, man. Tush. That isn't enough. Night air also you need. You must have several look-through-the-walls in your house. See—just like mine." He pointed. "Why, I felt even as ill as you, I tore this opening in my wall. Am I white and tremulous now, Chang Jwan?"

That's easily answered. "No," is the quickest to say.

All the villagers—for gossip thrives in the village—soon learned of Chang Jwan's strange illness, and of the remedy prescribed by Doctor Chen Twom. There was the tailor, illest of the ill. He couldn't talk, so he had to whisper, "Why should I pay Doctor Chen a grievous fee, merely to learn that I am white and tremulous, and should have a look-through-the-wall, as they call this new invention, in my house? Is it sensible to pay money to learn what I already know? I'll have in the carpenter, forthwith." Other sick persons in the village said precisely the same thing. They cut look-through-the-walls. And, in a month or two they were noticeably on the mend.

Doctor Chen Twom, brilliant man, said to himself, "This is queer business. I recommended the look-through-the-wall merely to aid Wing Dow in his elopement, so he could easier steal his bride. And lo—the look-through-the-wall becomes medicine. It good. Nearly as good as huo yao—*The* medicine. I shall list it in my book, under the caption, 'Highly Recommended.'"

King Chiah Djang, instead of playing po
lo, and making war, spent his waking hours
hunched over a chessboard. His palace was
chill, and damp, and gloomy. No wonder
he always felt on the verge of a seizure.
His physicians did their level best; and saw
their beards turn rapidly grey. For King
Chiah Djang invariably spoke his mind. He
said the palace physicians were noddies. And
he'd send for a dozen real doctors, men who
could put him in fettle.

With a written royal command in his
sleeve, Doctor Chen Twom entered the palace. He had the eye of one who knows. He
had the look of one who will not be gainsaid.
The king recognized these qualities. His
Majesty was quite civil. "Doctor Chen
Twom? The very man I want. It seems
you have invented a torn wall, which cure
you prescribe for just such ailings as mine."
Spoke the doctor, "Never do I claim credit,
when the credit belongs otherwhere. Your
Majesty refers to an invention which some
call 'look-through-the-wall,' but which I, in
my book, have named the 'wingdow.'" (We

call it window.) "This I did to honor the
inventor, a young village person, Wing Dow.
When Your Majesty is cured, you may praise
Wing Dow."

Instructed by Doctor Chen, the masons
chiseled large openings in the palace walls.
They let in air and light, into the throne-
room, the council chamber, into the king's
own tiring room. And the king gazed
through his wingdows and was surprised to
see the world so vast. More, he actually
went through a wingdow, and strolled in the
garden. Doctor Chen encouraged him in
this. History tells the result. King Chial
Djang recovered health.

When winter threw its snows upon the
garden, then, of course, the king stayed under
roof. But every day he sat close to a wing
dow and gazed upon the happenings outside
North wind, or west wind, he sat at his high
wingdow. "Kerchoo——"

While the palace physicians hustled him
to bed, His Majesty demanded that they
state the cause of his sudden illness. They
very eagerly, fixed the blame. "That villag

simpleton, that doctor—was his name Chen Twom? He is to blame. Your Majesty should sword him. He invented the look-through-the-wall, and Your Majesty sat in a draft, and now you have a bad cold." King Chiah Djang took another draught of gin seng, and he said to the physicians, "Chen Twom didn't invent it. A man named Wing Dow he mentioned as at fault. Director of Royal Safety, why are you not at my bed-stead head when I need you? Go bring me the man Wing Dow." The director replied, "Your Majesty, this Wing Dow knave is held by the Provincial Authorities. He is in jail for atrocious thievery. He stole a farmer's daughter, and took her to the Tumbled Mountains, and she can't be found. The Provincial Authorities will not willingly unlock their jail."

"Kerchoo," said the king. "What? Kerhoo. Haven't you gone to do as I ordered? Where is my curved sword?" But the director of royal safety had already looked to his own safety.

Sure enough, the Provincial Authorities

were stubborn. They insisted upon a paper of royal command. The director had no such paper. He dared not ask the king to write one. Cleverly he overrode the difficulty by stealing, in night, His Majesty's sword. When he placed the royal sword on a table in front of the Provincial Authorities, they saw the point. "We are persuaded," they said. "Take the man. Take two men. Empty our jail, if you wish."

By this time, the king, quite happily, had been relieved of his cold. He sat near a wingdow, thinking life pleasant. To see the director enter with a prisoner surprised him. "Where have you been so long, Director? What recreant, trembling in chains, do you bring?" "This, Your Majesty, is the man you wish beheaded. He is Wing Dow, inventor of look-through-the-walls." But the king merely smiled. "Dear. Dear. I have lost a good half of my displeasure. He is a scamp—true—yet, what is one scamp among so many? Give him a piece of gold, Director, and *let him run the gantlet.*"

A thousand soldiers fell in line on either

side of the garden walk. Their captains gave careful instructions. "Be graceful, men, and be strong. Remember, you are looked upon by His Majesty. Grasp your bamboos *so*, and flourish them behind your shoulders. Each of you wait until Wing Dow has run one pace beyond; then, strike him sharply. And, oh, men, let noise be in the blows, that the king may be pleased, and Wing Dow be punished." And that is running the gantlet.

The General of Ceremonies called up his deepest voice. "Soldiers, attention. . . . Ruffle the drums." Drumsticks danced on the taut tiger skins. "Remove chains." The iron links clattered in falling. Wing Dow stood unfettered. "Flourish bamboos." Gracefully, the soldiers waved their hand-staves. And Wing Dow, seeing, knew that he must surely die.

But the General of Ceremonies was swelling his chest in military greatness. "Prisoner. . . . *Go.*"

A head is precious when it is one's own. Wing Dow hurled himself away. He over-set the general, leapt clear of drums and fallen drummers. Like a hare cried up in the hunting field, he sped through the royal chrysanthemum beds, round the palace, away, —his heels a blur of forced motion. Count

But Wing Dow was . . . running, running, running . . .

one for Wing's first stride, then two,—and three was his disappearance.

The soldiers muttered, "This is no way to run the gantlet. He has misunderstood the rule. He goes the wrong direction." The general gasped, "After him, war-men. Catch the ignorant fellow."

But Wing Dow was far in the distance . . . running, running, running . . . toward the twilight-darkened mountains . . . to freedom . . . and the beautiful Seeah See See.

A GARDEN DOWN IN KIANG SING

AH KEE had only a garden, had only an acre garden, a well, a cottage . . . had a garden filled with flowers, a well of sweet water, a cottage with its three blue plates, a kettle, and maybe a chair. May Providence give us all wide fields and a softer bed than Ah Kee slept on. But we'll never see such flowers as his. The flowers of now are not the same that bloomed in Kiang Sing.

The people remarked, as people will, that Ah Kee was crazy. "Consider our neighbor boy, Ah Kee. Undoubtedly he suffers with fox-of-the-brain." (The doctors say a fox

is cause of madness.) "He has rich soil in
his acre garden. He could raise weigh-a-
pound radishes. He could become wealthy
by selling fatten-you melons. The earth is
fitted to produce gin seng, and that's a money
crop. But no. He starves amid the scented
beauty. Flowery starvation." Someone else
took up the complaint. "If I had a garden
of such strong soil I'd soon wear a coat with
a broidered back, instead of going half-bare
to the sun. A percipient person could make
a fortune every year between Ah Kee's four
high-built walls. But Ah Kee is crazy, and
his coat is a rag. I have seen him trade a
valuable melon for a pale blue flower. It
may be that he has made even worse bar-
gains."

The talk was unkind, but perfectly true—
in some particulars. Ah Kee *had* made many
a trade as bad, or not so good. Neighbor
and journey-goer alike had cheated him woefully. Through Kiang Sing lies a road of
far travel. The caravans wind down with
furs and tree-wax, with gem crystal and
white stone for the porcelain makers. They

return with mud idols and made silk. Going
or coming, they think of gain, for the caravan
men go a-travel for the sake of their purses.
Often Ah Kee would stand on the rim of the
road till a caravaneer stopped to chaffer.

"A turquoise, great rich man." (Spoken
to Ah Kee, so ragged and poor. But then,
the turquoise was contrived of glass.) "This
gem, one time, was the Amir's greatest joy.
Buy it, great man. The price is little." Ah
Kee had no interest in colored glass. "Have
you any flowers, traveler? Any peonies have
you, from the Yellow Lama's land? Any
rare lilies, or a blue-black rose?" "Rose or
lily, *I* don't know, but I have a flower . . .
bend closer to hear me . . . that bloomed in
a Shah's own garden. Is it likely to be common? Wait here till I come back with the
plant of royalty." The caravan man passed
down the line of his resting camels. From
the barter goods he took an empty crock.
He filled his crock with road earth, and into
the earth he thrust a chance-found twig.
Appearing half reluctant, he at length returned to Ah Kee and premonished him

"Never you tell anyone the story of this flower. The Shah reaches far to take vengeance. Had I been caught at the border, had this little plant been found in my goods . . . ah well, I was not caught. My head is with me, and the sword has lost a prize."

Ah Kee promised he would never tell, and he paid the price, without a word of "That's too high," though it was—unless perchance a penny crock is worth what it can hold of silver. And a month later Ah Kee was still wondering why his new plant remained dry and brown, when it should have been putting out wonderful amethystine, or possibly flame-dyed blossoms. And the twig had no more root than a beggar's walking-staff.

But Ah Kee was not always cheated. Often he secured really exceptional flowers. He doted on roses. Therein his good taste greatly aided his purse, for the rose has many table uses. The rose in a vase, that's a frequent sight, and there, in Kiang Sing, the people make rose sugar. They make rose oil, and they make rose dumplings. And they pay liberally for rose petals to mix with tea and give it the name it bears, Paradise Fragrance.

Seeds from Ah Kee's garden went to lands strange and far. The large plants he divided into many small ones, and they were carried by caravans, and they went in ships, I don't

The rose in a vase, that's a frequent sight.

know where. Sometimes a visitor came to say, "I want this. It is new to my sight." Once came a stranger of commanding, official look, to make a close search in the garden. He found a peony that made him buy. When he had gone, the neighbors came to babble. "Mercy me. Were you not frightened? That man serves the king, in Chang An City. Now you have gold, and will buy a new coat." "No," said Ah Kee, "I've still to pay for a shrub the caravan is bringing." And that helps explain why he remained so poor.

Another visitor to Ah Kee's garden was a mandarin's son, from the nearby town, named Hong Lok. (Hong Lok was the mandarin's son. The town was Shang Hin.) I have no compliments to bestow upon Hong Lok. His were evil ways. He threw stones at the idols, drank millet brandy (and don't forget the sam shu), played with spotted little cubes—dice, they are called—always shouted loudest at the cricket fights, took what he pleased from any man, and laughed at the wailing. Think of Hong Lok as one very bad.

Let's see what happened. The mandarin's son needed crickets to train for a fight he had determined to win. Accompanied by friends and servants, he roamed the fields, overturning stones in his search. As ill-luck ordered, he came to the wall surrounding Ah Kee's garden. He motioned a hand to his servants, and they threw themselves in a heap against the wall. Upon their piled-up

Upon their piled-up bodies stepped the rich one, and stood gazing into Ah Kee's garden.

bodies stepped the rich one and stood gazing into Ah Kee's garden. Ah Kee bowed very low and said, "I feel greatly honored that your highness condescends to notice my sorry property." The mandarin's son, of course, paid no attention to him. Hong Lok reached over and grasped a rose. Away from the bush skipped a fine large cricket. "Hi. There's a cricket," exclaimed the young man. "A cricket, I say, you louts. Over the wall with you and catch him." Up and over came the servants. This way and that they swarmed through the flowers. Ah Kee ran after them. "Gentlemen. Gentlemen. Please, will you stop? Dear me to goodness, my dragon-blood rose is broken. Gentlemen, pray—oh, my gloxinias. Gentlemen, pray forego—oh, my goldylocks. Gentlemen, pray forego your tiger-after-deer-like chase. Now, Kwan Yin have pity. There falls the peony I. . . ." The mandarin's son turned his quick fury upon Ah Kee. "Don't make such noise, you stretch-mouth imbecile. Your raucous utterances will scare the cricket dead. Have you never learned there's courtesy to be served a well-born visitor?"

Perhaps Ah Kee lacked daring. At any

rate he didn't do the thing he wished. He didn't grasp the over-fat bully and tear the life from his throat. As calm-eyed as the village idol, in subdued voice he acknowledged his mistake. "Alas, I have done the unpardonable. I didn't recognize your superior person. Pray walk where you will within this garden, which grows each moment brighter under your worship's heel."

For a very good reason, the superior person and his servants immediately scrambled back over the wall. The cricket had escaped through a chink between bricks. And he was a desirably large cricket, well worth following into the field beyond. Ah Kee was left alone to mourn the despoilment.

Heavy hearted, and eyes dimmed, the boy hastened afar from his ravaged garden. He couldn't bear the sight. Goolah. Listen. . .

Next morning in the early hours Ah Kee took up a rake to smooth away the traces of his great disaster. But the earth he found level. No heavy boot marks showed. His flowers stood soldierly upright. They seemed to be in a greater numbers than before. A

Kee began to think he had been too hasty
in his fears. There was no damage. The
flowers were entire. Not a blossom drooped
where the visitors of yesterday had tramped.
Good. But very strange.

The mandarin's son and his bottle com-
panions were out to make high holiday.
"Let's fish," said one. "Let's dice," said one.
"Let's go to the garden we visited last day.
I lost my knife and I think it is there."
"And we'll put a stick to the insolent
gardener's back." "Agreed. The common
people are growing too impudent. It's a
duty to teach them respect."

Say a pity for Ah Kee, alone against many.
He knew his strength could never overthrow
even one of the intruders. To ask the neighbors for aid would be foolish. The people
round about stood in fear of the mandarin.
They wouldn't dare say "Boo" to his son.
The magistrate was far away, and worse—
beholden to the rich man. No help for it.
Ah Kee from a distance watched his enemies
search amid the flowers. He saw Hong Lok
grasp a rose to break it. He heard a roar

of pain. He saw the others gather to their
leader. They made loud noises of anger.
Presently they raised their clubs and began
to strike the flowers. Like scythemen going
through a harvest field, they swung their
clubs, and the blossoms fell.

No one weeps forever. Ah Kee at last
raised his face from the earth. He beheld a
young lady of much beauty. On a day long
before, she had come to his garden, and he
remembered that she had a great interest for
peonies.

"Your ladyship finds me in sorrow," said
Ah Kee. "The flowers I promised cannot be
given. They have been destroyed by a mandarin evil-doer."

"No matter," said the lady. "I shan't
need them. My garden is now over-thronged
with flowers. I should like to dispose of the
ones too many."

Ah Kee, for the first time noticed that she
had a dwarf peony in her slender hand. It
was very tiny, toy size, in a porcelain jar
that might have been small for a thimble.
The boy at once offered to buy. "It's a

h Kee for the first time noticed that she had a dwarf peony
in her slender hand.

Fairy's Blush. I'll take it, gladly. Pray
wait till I get money from the house."

But the vanity of man caused Ah Kee to
peer in a mirror. His face was clay streaked;
it looked like the face of a soldier in war
time. He changed color as he remembered
how the beautiful lady had smiled. A vig-
orous rubbing kept him longer than he reckoned in the house.

The lady had vanished. In her stead were
flowers. The garden was filled with the
beauty of old. Ah Kee rushed to the gate.
He saw only a neighbor, only a man of the
village. "Where is the lady? She left before I could pay her for the flowers."

"No lady has passed this way within the
past hour," answered neighbor villager. "I
must think you have been asleep," said the
gardener.

"But then, of course, she was in a sedan
chair. Which road did the chair bearers
take?" "No lady. No chair. No bearers.
Nothing within the last hour." "You saw
no servants with flowers—a thousand serv-

ants placing flowers in my garden? Only a thousand could fill it so quickly."

The old man shook his head. "Poor boy, so sadly deluded. There was no lady. No servants brought flowers. Your flowers are destroyed, Ah Kee. Can you understand? I was a witness to the destruction. Your garden is bare." Then a breeze swung the garden gate. The neighbor's eyes snapped wide. "I, too, am crazy," he exclaimed. "Now by every shen that rides the wind, I'm seeing flowers where no flowers are. Alas, the fox has entered my mind. I'm the craziest man I ever knew." He went away holding his head.

Ah Kee was still seeking the beautiful lady, when those terrible men, the "high hats,"—the ting chai,—the yamen runners, arrived. The mandarin's son was close behind them, pointing. "There he stands, bold in his evilness. Seize him, before he breaks more of the king's peace and wounds more of the king's subjects." The high-hatted lictors performed the act of seizure, which in-

cluded much shaking, and many strokes with
bamboos. Ah Kee lost grasp of his money.
Coppers flew in the six directions. The lictors
promptly let go of their prisoner and con-
tended for the coins. It was good fortune
for them; good, too, for Hong Lok, the mandarin's son. "A-ha. He tries to bribe the
high-hats. There is another serious crime.
Be sure to list it against him."

Hong Lok was much pleased with himself.
But his pleasure turned to amazement when
he entered Ah Kee's garden. What could
have revived the flowers he had beaten down?
Had he imagined the destruction? Hong
Lok bared his arm and saw a long red
scratch upon it. That was proof he had not
imagined.

"Hadn't we better go away, before the
magic strikes us?" inquired a follower.

"Nonsense," roared Hong Lok. "What
magic would dare strike me? Get to work,
you idle-bones. Dig up the flowers, and prepare this land for decent farming."

Still the follower had fears. "Hadn't we
better wait until you receive the papers giv-

ing full possession? This is magic, I'm sure, and some of the witnesses may suffer with trembles and give poor testimony."

Hong Lok held to his purpose. Again he exposed the scratch upon his arm, and said in his side-of-the-mouth talk. "Here is the wound received in this garden. Ah Kee is responsible. He must pay with his property for the hurt. Don't worry over witnesses. The magistrate has long guzzled my wine; therefore will decide as I have told him to do—witness or no witness." Up rushed another recreant servant and said, "Beat me, master, for I shall dig no more. The flowers are changing to faces, and that is witch-work." The others, too, were shaking. So Hong Lok used his surest persuasion upon them. "I'll give a prize to him who drinks the most sam shu in the fewest minutes. Fill up, men. Sam shu and fear never keep house together." The jugs were quickly emptied. Then the staggering servants again took up their hoes to dig.

All this time the sky had been darkening. Black clouds rimmed with a sulphury yellow

came past at tree-top height. Moving in
whirls a cold wind blustered up—a yang
chiao feng—a ram's horn wind. It laid hold
on the flower petals and carried them round
and round, more of them and more, till the
air was filled as with a snow. These signs
despite, Hong Lok continued in his folly.
"Sing, men, sing. Out with a jolly worded
song. We'll dance to shake off the cold."

"Please stop," said a pleasant voice from
aside. "You and your men are breaking my
flowers. You must stop at once, for my
people grow very angry." Hong turned, and
his narrow eyes beheld a beautiful lady. He
bowed unsteadily and reached to break a
poppy stem. The wickedly smiling lout offered his gift to the lady. "A flower for
your hair, my child. Take it, girl. When
Hong Lok offers flowers, that's a compliment."

The flower in his hand began to writhe.
The stem split open for half of its length.
It grew a coat of workman's blue. A hand
appeared where the blossom had been. Hong
Lok held in his hand a little old man of the

spirit world. It was a flower-gnome, rapidly growing, and shrieking hate.

The terrified youth released his grasp. So much the worse to do. Sharp little fingers raked his cheek. He closed his eyes and ran.

Elsewhere were other gnomes, dozens clinging to every man; scratching and thumping Hong Lok's servants. Lightnings raced crookedly through the overhead storm. Close thunders shook the earth. The wind changed for colder. It was a demon's play time in the garden of Ah Kee.

Howling for mercy, the terrified servants sought to escape. Blinded, they ran in circles, at last to find the walls, to clamber over and run again, crashing through woods and thickets, through vines that choked and briars that tore. They were scattered miles apart when the thunder rumbles died away and the darkness passed.

That evening in the house of the law, His Honor grew impatient. "The trial is too long delayed. Lictors, did you look in all ponds for the chief complaining witness?"

The lictors replied, "Please, Your Honor,

we searched hereabout and thereabout, in ponds and brooks, low in wells and high in trees, but everywhere we looked he wasn't there. Hong Lok was too far to find."

"Then let the next highest witness give testimony," commanded the judge.

Up rose a bandaged man and said, "I know only this. I drank sam shu. Something happened. Now I am aching in many bandages, tied with red strings to keep demons away." The other witnesses made statements precisely similar. They took care not to mention Ah Kee. They thought he might not like it if talked about. He might again summon his flower demons.

The magistrate hardly knew what to do. His decision had been written some time ago. On paper he had awarded his friend Hong Lok a garden that once belonged to Ah Kee. Ah Kee he had sentenced to an age in the cells. But now he was not so sure of his wisdom. His Honor knew something of demons and their rages.

Into the court came a man with bells.

A magistrate holds a fairly high rank, but what's a little magistrate compared to a man with bells, from Chang An City. Chang An is the capital city. The exalted person— and he was fourth assistant secretary to the comptroller of the four eminences, scowled, and turned a circle, to see if all were bowing. Then words burst from his lips. "You must put a stop to the too bad weather in this magistracy. I was delayed in a terrible hail, a surprise storm. Where is one named Ah Kee, grower of peonies in a garden?"

The magistrate's eyes were a-blink. To save his back from the cruel bamboo, his thoughts came quickly. "Ah Kee? Oh, yes, Sir, Ah Kee. You mean the boy, Ah Kee. Ah Kee, in an accident, thrust his head through a cangue" (prisoner's collar). That was a wholly false statement; yet he said it as innocently as a little cat says "Meewyl." "We shall endeavor to remove the cangue immediately. I hope you have no charges against Ah Kee."

"Charges? Of course I have. I must

charge Ah Kee faithfully to observe this commission from Her Majesty, The Queen, may she live forever."

Hong Lok closed his eyes and ran.

In the royal commission Ah Kee was appointed Gardener-at-a-distance. His dutie were simple. He had to send a dozen rar peonies every year to Her Majesty's repre

sentative, the Intendant of The Everbloom-
ing Gardens. He was privileged to wear 7th
rank embroidery, but I grieve to say, never
saved enough money to buy it. He continued to spend all income upon flowering
plants . . . and was quite happy. Only one
thing ever distressed him. Occasionally a
wild man, most likely insane, would peep
over the garden wall and scream, "Let go
of me, you flower demons," and then run
howling into Hu Pei forest.

THE PICTURE PRINCESS

In that ancient book, the Meng Nai Shu, is a very cryptic statement. "The Princess Wan·Erh gathered berries, and made a rabbit."

Mmmmmmm. Made a rabbit do *what?*

The Shih Kwo is a slightly larger book. It adds five words to the rabbit. "The Princess Wan Erh gathered berries, and made a rabbit. . . . thereby inventing the first picture."

Nothing more.

In the market square sits old Kung Lin

the story-teller. So I've sold my Meng Nai Shu, and my Shih Kwo book. I, too, sit in the market square, and say, "That dragon was fierce, indeed. Now tell about the Picture Princess."

King Yueh Wee was sonless, yet he smiled and knew contentment. His small daughter, Princess Wan Erh, kept his heart from vain longings. The princess also kept her father excited, and interested, and wondering what would happen next. Wan Erh, royal princess, had been given great beauty. Her voice was like the little feng ling, the wind-bells which make music on the eaves of the palace. She had graces. She could sew a seam with no straggling and bewilderment of thread. She played upon the tung wood scholar's-lute, and sang the song "My Beautiful Jade Needle," prettiest, strangest, most rememberful song of all.

The princess loved to ramble in the many-cred garden. Every day in pleasant weather of the summer she soldiered the nurses into one. And while she skipped and led the march, the nurses, each wheeling a barrow of toys, dashed under the fragrant paulownia trees and under the calycanthus, striving vainly to keep near the royal small mistress.

Wan Erh found a bush of ripened berries. Those were pretty berries, gay in their fullest coloring. When squeezed between fingers, they dripped purple. The princess said to her favorite nurse, to her who carried the fan, "I like these. They have wine—only thicker. Let's squeeze them." The nurse answered, "Please, Your Highness, I think they are make-death berries. I am afraid." But the princess already had two hands filled. "The men drink wine. The chancellor drinks barrels. I think I shall crush these berries for their wine, and the wine will be for the dolls. Though they shan't have much. If they fall over—like the chancellor—you are to put them back in their chairs."

So the princess extracted wine. She gave a drink to every doll—rather too hurriedly for in the end each doll had a purple head. The favorite nurse said, "I think you are hurting their looks." Wan Erh herself was dissatisfied. "They are blushing. The imagine a prince is hidden in the oleanders, watching. Seat that tipsy thing back in her chair, nurse. No doubt for her I'll have a doctor's bill to pay."

Queen Nan Ling, upon the palace portico, raised her voice high in a summons. The sound was jumbled and indistinct when it reached the berry gatherers, far in the garden. But Princess Wan Erh knew every word of it. She had heard the same call so many, many times. "Wan Erh, where are you? Oh, my child, to play the banjo you must come now, and to spell the foreign languages, and take your lesson in embroidery." Wan Erh murmured against the commandation. 'There's Mu Tsing (Mother) calling. I knew she would. Wants me to be a truly finished princess. Work. Work. Work. Dear! Dear! All princess and no play is hard on a body." Away dashed the Princess Wan Erh, dissatisfied, but going.

The favorite nurse, with long fan trailing, kept close behind. (The others, wheel-barrow-hindered, could come as their breaths would let them.) In the plaisance, where it

has the marble paving, Princess Wan Erh
dropped her wine. The bottle, on the marble, went into unnumbered pieces. Wan Erh
took a rather sober view of the damage. She
had to pause to think of good words to express her disapproval. She was not one of
those people who rush their words without
thinking. She thought of "Ai yu," which is
a symbol for sorrow, but never spoke it. Instead she pointed to a purple stain upon the
pave and said, "Look, Nurse. What is that?"

The nurse glanced downward. "Please, it
is spilt berry color. I mean it is 'wine' upon
the marble. Or something else, if you've
changed your mind."

Wan Erh said, "You always say such droll
things—not a bit what you mean. It is a
rabbit, of course. Almost. See. It looks
like a rabbit. This ear should be longer."
She used a finger to make it longer. "This
leg needs a foot." She gave it a foot. "His
whiskers are one-sided." She made them
two-sided. "Now. There's a very true rabbit, except for his color—and this is really
an improvement. Why, rabbits are easy.

believe I could make another. Let me have *your* bottle of berry paint, please."

"It is a rabbit, of course."

Queen Nan Ling instructed an outside musician to blow the special "Come" upon a bugle. The bugler blew until he fell exhausted.

Princess Wan Erh practised every day. With the aid of the nurses she discovered many new colors. She covered the white stone terrace with elephants, and lesser beasts and birds. The gardeners thought surely they would be worked to death with so much mopping to do. Dull fellows. Unappreciative of the new art.

King Yueh Wee inquired of his master-of-household. "Why are the towels so scandalously marked? Towels, by nature white, I find covered with red and green and blue." The master-of-household stammered, "The . . . She . . . You . . . I. . . . They are indeed marked with color, Your Majesty. There must be a cause." He didn't dare say the princess was guilty. The king frowned. In his bear's-growl voice he said, "Then discover the cause. And see that these colors come out. Else you'll require a new head." The king could be stern when need came.

When next Princess Wan Erh saw the master-of-household she instantly noticed his noisy distress. She said, "Why are you weeping, Master-of-household? Did the cook fly into anger and break another vinegar jug?"

Master-of-household replied, "I weep because my eyes are flooding. I'll not be here much longer, Highness. His Majesty has warned me." Poor chap, he broke down completely.

Wan Erh asked "Why?" She kept on asking "Why?" until she got an answer. Then she went to the king.

The Princess Wan Erh said to Yueh Wee, her father, "Daddy, I don't want the master-of-household to lose his head. He is so jolly and temper-keeping. He gives me the ripest peaches, and laughs deliciously when I toss the seeds, so hard to find, deep in the shun swe carpets. Besides, *I* put the color marks on the towels. I am painting."

The king asked, "What? What's *that?* What *is* painting?"

Wan Erh informed him, "Why, I make colored marks, and they become rabbits, and birds, and various things. Quite pretty. Next, I shall paint you—your side face.

That is best—more kingly than the view with both ears showing."

The king, somewhat alarmed, cried against it. "No. No. It might be hurtful to my dignity. The subjects might laugh if they saw me with a colored face." (He didn't understand at all.) "Paint the chancellor. Paint him green. Ho. Ho. Ho. Green."

The chancellor, half-dozing, half-opened his eyes. "What's that? How do you say? Your Majesty's green jade bracelet is on the tiring-room table." He had been after the wine again.

So Wan Erh fetched her fir-flower tablet and her brushes and her pots of paints. She commanded the old chancellor, "Hold your chin up out of your coat, please. And rub your eyes into brightness." The chancellor obeyed. He sat blinking, trying to straighten his mind.

When the princess finished the picture she displayed it to the chancellor. "There. That's you."

The man was horrified. It was the very

"Hold your chin up out of your coat, please!"

first picture he had seen. "Why, that's myself—upon a flimsy paper. I'll fall. I'll fall. Let me help you hold myself up." He tried to get out of the chair. But he couldn't. He couldn't lift a heel, couldn't lift a hand, nor one of its five divisions. His much wine-tippling finally had brought upon him the immovability called "paralysis."

Doctors and wise-men consulted, smiling or frowning, and stretching their words. King Yueh Wee demanded, "What is the trouble? Why doesn't the chancellor arise and go about his work?"

The wise-men replied, "We are agreed, all save a few imbeciles, that the so-called 'picture' is to be blamed for the chancellor's motionless sitting here. No man can be in two places at one time—without magic. Hence, if the chancellor be in his chair; and be also upon a paper, then he is divided. In the division he has been injured. That part of him upon paper must be given back to that part of him within the chair." So the paper part of the chancellor was pasted upon the chair part. But no good came. With himself to aid himself he was still unable to walk.

The king said to Wan Erh, "Daughter, don't again paint the chancellor. And don't paint me. Especially me. Don't paint the army. Don't paint the cook. Paint nobody. The doctor says a person painted cannot walk." Wan Erh sighed. "Very well, Daddy; though I can't think my painting is wholly to blame for the chancellor's stepless-ness. I painted the *doctor* a day ago, and there he walks to the treasury."

Wan Erh owned a rabbit. He was a rab-bit, plain and simple, of the common, or gardener's vexation variety; with ears no longer than usual, and legs no shorter. He lived outside in a pen, until the princess lugged him off to her room of the bed, the dolls, and hide-from-the-world. When the door was safely fastened, Wan Erh said, "I think the doctors had little to do. Painting doesn't hurt anyone—at least I don't see how it could. I shall paint rabbit. If he can't move when I have finished, I shall give him to the cook. He is fat . . . the rabbit . . .

not the cook; though the cook is too. Here
are cabbage leaves, rabbit. Sit quietly, and
be your prettiest self."

For a long time the rabbit refused to be
still. He was amid strangeness, and he
wanted to see. He sat down once, but just
as the princess began to paint him, the guards
were changed below. That meant a long
while of drum-given noises. The princess
kept patience. She waited until rabbit settled down again. Then she painted him.
The rabbit slept. He never dreamed of what
was soon to happen.

The princess to herself explained, "If this
rabbit, my subject, *can* move, now that he
is painted, then he *must* move. If he *does*
move, then the painting hasn't hurt him. . . .
Let's see whether he sits, or goes." She
lighted a firecracker. The burning spluttered
on through the fuse, into the paper tube—
where it touched the powder.

And the painting hadn't hurt the rabbit
at all. Neither had the explosion, but rabbit
wouldn't believe it. He blundered against
the oo ni yao vases. They were porcelain

vases, easy to break. They added to rabbit's eagerness to go. Out he went—through the five-sided window.

And the painting hadn't hurt the rabbit at all.

The pitiful chancellor was seated in the courtyard. Woe, it filled his thoughts. He couldn't walk. He must quietly sit his life away. Very sad.

A terrible explosion came to his ears.

They, the ears, were not paralyzed. The chancellor gazed upward. His beard pointed skyways, in resemblance to a steeple. So it seems his neck was not very paralyzed either. The chancellor gazed at Princess Wan Erh's five-sided window. He saw something leap out of the window. He saw a huge creature —perfectly wild—with wide-open mouth— with claws out-stretched—sailing down upon him.

The chancellor was paralyzed. Quite true. But the chancellor arose, and he shrieked, and went his way. And the people who saw him murmured, "Look. Can't he run? That man, whoever he may be, surely, is training himself to be a king's messenger."

King Yueh Wee was delighted to see his chancellor moving once more. He told Wan Erh, "You may paint again—but be careful. I shouldn't paint any really important persons. Paint only those who don't matter." So the princess painted in peace. It was no longer necessary to work behind a fastened door. And by the way, the rabbit wasn't hurt in the slightest. He had descended lightly, upon the chancellor.

If I have not said the king was rather fleshy, I'll say it now. He was. After exercising briskly he had trouble to get his breath. Every time he rode po lo, or ran with a kite, or skipped the rope, he puffed and wheezed extravagantly. The physicians plenipotentiary gave him gin seng and brayed toad-claws, and he promptly went worse. The more they gave him ko fen, the more he wheezed. Finally, the oldest doctor opened his medicine book at random and read what he found, "Salt. His Majesty needs salt in his breath. He must breathe the air of the sea." The king demurred, "I do not like a rocking, toss-you boat. A boat is too unsteady." The doctor read his book again, "The salty air is necessary, but the boat is not. Your Majesty may have a bridge built upon the ocean." The king was delighted. He gave orders to the royal engineers. They rushed the work under sun and moon.

Unfortunately, King Yueh Wee forgot to

ask permission for the building of his bridge. He was a king upon the land—but only a man upon the ocean. The Shen of the Sea chanced to spy the bridge. They howled. They were angry. "What is this? And why? We have given no permission. We have received no tribute from the king. Yet, he clutters our sea with a building." They went at the bridge most vengefully. They were very strong fellows, those Shen.

The Princess Wan Erh sometimes painted her pictures hurriedly. Now and then she left out the unimportant details. Details are bothersome anyhow. So, when the princess painted the Sea Bridge, just before its destruction, she neglected to paint the pillars which held it aloft. King Yueh Wee saw this picture, and marvelled greatly. "A bridge supported by the air. Excellent. I must speak to the dragon, Liang Loong."

Liang Loong was a Superior Dragon of the sky. A superior dragon has all the gifts of a lesser shen. In fact, he can change himself to a shen—though he seldom does—because a dragon has claws for fighting, and a shen has not. The Superior Dragon said, "Certainly, I'll give permission, give material aid, too,—do more than that, and myself build the bridge. But wait. . . . I have heard that in the kingdom are persons who take the look and the strength of a man and place it upon paper. Whereupon the man is unable to move. . . ."

The king interrupted, "That is called 'painting.' But it is harmless. The chancellor wouldn't move merely because he was lazy."

"Perhaps. Perhaps," quoth the dragon. "But you must lay down a law with such frequent mention of the headsman that no one will dare to paint *me*. And let no one paint my dragon mate. Else there'll be gnashing of teeth, and clashing of arms, and lashing from battle to battle."

The king said, "Of course not. They shan't do so. I'll write a law a whole ream long." He promptly instructed Princess Wan Erh not (no matter how much she wished) to paint (no matter how the chancellor had recovered) the dragon.

The air was noisy with the beat of dragon wings. The accommodating dragons carried ropes to the sky and hooked them into the firmament. In the slightest little more than no time they had a bridge hung over the sea.

King Yueh Wee at once began to improve. He rode daily upon the bridge, and flung empty litchee shells at the howling Shen of the Sea so far below. He could laugh without wheezing. And the Shen could howl, but nothing more do in vengeance.

A tragedy was in the making. *The dragon's mate fell ill.* The anxious Liang Loong inquired, "Can you lift your feet?"

The other answered, "No."

"Can you flutter a wing?"

"No." Then the dragon roared like powder in a gun. "The king has broken his promise. You have been painted. Your strength for motion has been put upon a paper. The king shall suffer for this outrage. I'll make an end to him, and all the royal family." But first, the dragon cut the ropes, and the bridge splashed into the sea. Only by chance King Yueh Wee had stayed at home that day, to check the chancellor at chess.

No one could doubt that the dragon was angry. King Yueh Wee guessed the trouble. He summoned his princess daughter. "Wan Erh, did you paint the dragon—or his mate?"

"No. No. No, Daddy. I have painted, since you told me not to paint dragons, only the gardener and still things—the cook, the army, an apple tree—no dragons."

The king said, "I'm glad you didn't; though it makes no difference now. The dragon thinks he has been painted, and that's enough. He will eat us to death if he can. Be very careful where you ramble. And if you see the dragon prowling outside—paint him. Picture him as paltry as he is."

Charms were distributed around the palace. The best magicians were ordered to come from their caves and help make the king's wide dwelling a peril to the furious Liang Loong.

Outside the royal garden was a swamp with a stream running through. Princess Wan Erh often went there to paint eels and

ibises. One day as she sat motionless in the
shadows, waiting for something she could
paint to come . . . what should appear but
the dragon. The Loong hunched up in the
swamp to wait. He was there on malice
bent. He intended to hide till he saw
the king come out for an evening canter
Then would be the opportunity.

Wan Erh had forgotten her father's warning. Instead of slipping quietly away, she
dabbled her brushes. There she sat, close
to the treacherous Loong, and painted his
picture. But for a few of the spikes on his
back she painted him completely. The
longer she looked at the creature, the more
ridiculous he appeared, a most amusing
monstrosity. She tried to hide laughter behind her hands, but they alas, were small.
The dragon heard.

The Loong rolled his eyes to gaze. His
forked tongue flicked out. He roared a note
of triumph. So the treacherous king's daugh
ter had come to be eaten. Ha. It would
be vengeance and profit at the same mouth
ful. He lifted a foot—but only a little way
His foot seemed to be trapped. Then th

dragon saw Wan Ehr's tablet, with his own likeness upon it. He knew that the worst had happened. His strength and beauty had been transferred to paper. He had met the chancellor's fate. Again he roared, lugubriously, and sat there, sinking in heart and body.

That evening the army moved to attack. The soldiers threw their several spears, they placed mouths of guns against the Loong, they hacked with swords—and the Loong lay quietly enough. But when they emptied crocks of hot oil, and the oil seeped between his scales, then the dragon was pained exceedingly. Forgetting that he had been painted, he made a prodigious effort to escape. His feet came up from the mud— for it was merely the mud that had ginned him. He was free to fight, or to go. And he didn't fight, so he must have gone. It's a very good thing he was painted when he was, because he never came back to have his vengeance.

As a princess, Wan Erh found the world quite pleasant, striving to be its best: but as an artist, she often said, "How stupid."

All the people had heard of the chancellor's misfortune, and they firmly believed it had been caused by the picture. They simply wouldn't be painted; neither for "Please," nor a penny. So Wan Erh never again pictured men on her tablet. She painted ships, and sheep, and sheldrakes—but not the people. And cabbages, and cockatoos—but not the king.

THE TELLTALE CHALK

In Kiang Sing, when a son is born, the
excited father hangs a bow—not a ribbon
bow, but a deadly bow of warfare—upon the
left side of his door. The neighbors pass,
and they see the bow—for eyes are sharp in
Kiang Sing. The neighbors remark, "Ah. A
bow for a fighting man. There's a warrior
in the house of Chang. Now our land is
safe against invasion. Bring drums and let
us make a glad noise beneath Chang's window. Salute the new son in the house."

Rumble and boom. Strike faster. Here comes Shang, the fiddler.

On the other hand, when a girl is born, Mr. Chang hangs cloth of silk upon the right side of his big red door. Along come the neighbors and see, and say. "Cloth for a weaver. How fortunate. Chang at last has a Thousand Pieces of Gold (daughter). Chang has a beautiful weaver in his house. Fetch gongs, and let us put our rejoicing into music." Clong. Clong. Frighten the demons, once and for all. Pay honor to Chang's little daughter. Such are the customs in Kiang Sing.

Now the man Wong Chi was a dweller in Kiang Sing. Seldom indeed it was that Wong Chi's rice pot boiled over on the kang. By that you are to know Wong Chi was in poverty. When a son came to Chi's house the father said, "What now? It's dreadful to be so short of copper. I can't even buy a bow for my child." But shortly his despair went from him, for he hit on a cleverness. "A make-believe bow will serve. I have some chalk. If my hand is not too unsteady, the neighbors shall yet see good news on my door." He used the chalk to picture a bow upon the left half of his door.

The neighbors are always alert for news. Old men left their crops in the fields, to come and blink at Wong Chi's door. Opinions wide apart were heard. "Why, it's merely a chalk picture. A false bow. That's bad. A false bow for a false warrior. Bad luck. Bad luck." Another cried, "Shame upon such false reasoning. Why talk nonsense? Chalk is for shoes and writing. Wong Chi's son will be a bootman, or else a scholar, with a leaning to military history." So they squabbled and pummeled their drums till demons for a mile around took fear and went into hiding.

The son was given "Ah Woy" for a name. When he came to be two years old (which would be only one year with us; because in Kiang Sing they add a year for good measure), as I say, when two years old he was given the test for the future. The astrologer came to make predictions. "I shall need," said the astrologer, "a piece of silver," (of course he would) "a cake of ink, a spear, a red jewel, a hoe. . . ." Ah Woy's father said, "I am a poor man. Do not frown so heavily, honorable astrologer. Few men are my superiors in poverty. I have no silver, no ink, no spear. As for jewels—*well*. Therefore, we must use make-believes. Here is a brick. Let it represent wealth. Let this piece of chalk be ink. A bamboo pole will do for a spear. For a hoe, why not use my hat?"

The astrologer finally consented, though he talked long upon the desirability of silver. The brick, the chalk, the bamboo, the hat, other things were placed in front of Ah Woy. And Ah Woy laid hands on the chalk. The astrologer said that the sign fitted in well with his other calculations. "Don't sell him. This chooser of chalk will make his mark in the world. He will keep the ancestral graves in repair, and be a credit to village and family." Thus spoke the astrologer, although he must have known he'd likely wait years for his fee.

It was a good prognostication. Wong Chi was proud of his famous-to-be son. He tied a piece of chalk to the boy's neck-string. The neck-string is a red cord, worn by every boy in Kiang Sing, to baffle ill-intentioned demons.

So utterly proud was Wong Chi that he worked doubly hard. His fortune changed. Meat came to his table. He had a few cash to spend for books. He sent Ah Woy to the village school.

Ah Woy took to his book with a vim. He would twirl the chalk on the end of his string and shriek whole pages, whole hours (they always study aloud in Kiang Sing). Only once did he fail. His necklace was taken by the schoolmaster. He was lost without his chalk to twirl. He couldn't think. He looked at a word and said of it "Chalk," though plain as day it was "Bob-tailed dragon," whose characters so utterly differ from written chalk, that the schoolmaster, though he was a learned man, and I'm perfectly for him, felt it necessary to take up his stick and make all the many strokes of Bob-tailed dragon on Ah Woy's back; and this he promptly set about to do, but the sentence is long enough, and should be stopped, forthwith and at once.

Most of Ah Woy's whippings were gained for making marks; not high marks in school, but Fu marks (Fu for good luck and happiness), upon the walls and paving. Every new stone he came to he gave a touch of chalk. It became an unbreakable habit.

Springs and autumns passed. Ah Woy journeyed to the capital. Inspectors went over him carefully. "Is that a writing on your coat?" "No. No. Honorable Inspector, it is only a grass stain." "That may be, but true or not, you must give up the coat." They opened the soles of his boots, prying for hidden papers. They scrutinized his chalk very closely. "Break it," said one. They broke it, but found nothing hidden. At last, when the searchers were sure that the boy had no books concealed, and so could not cheat, they led him to a bare small room.

Ah Woy sat down to write. In thousands of other tiny rooms were thousands of other young scholars, and grandfather scholars; some writing with assurance, others already crazy and weeping. This was in the Hall of Examination. Three days passed. Ah Woy came out into the sunshine. He rested a short time. Then he returned to the examination cell for another three days of thought and writing. Nine days he spent in solitude. It was finished. Ah Woy would graduate and become a great man. How pleasant. Or he would fail, and the villagers would jeer and point him out as a horrible example —a failure.

The Chief Examiner was in a bad humor. His eyes were wearied with much reading. Papers littered table and floor. "What idiots the young people of today are," growled the Examiner. And those are familiar words. "Here's one who writes Chueh for Chieh— and no doubt expects to pass. I'll bet he's a native of Kiang Sing. The people of Kiang Sing are dolts. They sent me not a single present." He threw the paper aside. Another hopeful scholar had failed.

The Examiner had a habit of talking to himself. "Here's still another imbecile. Doesn't know enough to keep his writing brush pointed. Slovenly. What's this white Fu on his paper? Chalk? That reminds

Papers littered table and floor.

me." The discontented Examiner arose and went to the door. "Ping Kew," he called to his servant, "put plenty of chalk on the soles of my boots. I expect to play chess in the palace this evening. My boot soles must be well whited." A wind swept in from the courtyard. The wind sent papers flying. A red examination paper marked with "Good Fortune" in chalk, descended upon the little heap of Honorably Graduated.

The Examiner made sure that his servant really intended to put good looks upon the boots. Once more he turned to the reading. "Here's another Wu Ta Lang. Writes with a split brush. There's nothing in this essay my heart can warm to. What stupid scholars."

Ah Woy lingered in the capital city. He could not eat. He could not sleep. His hands twitched, and his head throbbed. Would the names never be posted? Ah. At last came news. Young men raced down the Street of Anxious Scholars. Ah Woy ran with them. He fought to gain a place close to the notices. Perhaps his name would be there—in characters of gilded ink.

Near to the village of Ah Woy's home stood a large and prosperous city. The young man had no work to do—not for the while. Often he strolled in the city. He saw new sights, had his wonder excited, but met no high adventure till he chanced within the street of the silk merchants. There he espied a beautiful girl, of an age he reckoned not greater than his own. When her sedan chair moved off he followed. Not once it occurred to him he might be doing wrong. For Ah Woy was smitten, and a young man smitten goes without a thought of "Should I so?"

The sedan stopped in a doorway. The young lady entered her home. Ah Woy was grieved to see that the house exactly resembled all other houses to which it was neighbor. There was not a brick's difference in half a hundred buildings. Still, that was a little thing. Ah Woy had his chalk. He made a bold mark on the door, and sauntered off, singing the song of "Lan who followed where his love led." This was in the Street of The Dwellers in Happiness.

A man came out of the house, and he noticed the mark on his door. Said he, "A thief has marked my house for an evil to be done. But two can play at marking. That thief will have a puzzled head when he returns to rob." The man of the house took chalk, and went from door to door. Each door he marked precisely as his own was marked. *A hundred doors were chalked with "Fu."* Again each house in the street exactly resembled its neighbor.

Ah Woy, at home, spoke to his honorable father. "My father, I'm a graduate. In a little while I shall go to some high office, and I'd like to go as a married man. Will you give me permission to marry a girl of my own choosing?" His father replied, "That's an unusual request. Howbeit, you've always been a son obedient. Yes, marry the maid you've come to love. I'll bargain with a go-between." Oh, fortunate day. Oh, joyful Ah Woy.

He who would marry and the go-between (the arranger of marriages), walked in the street of The Dwellers in Happiness. "This is the house, honorable Go-between. Here is the mark made with chalk upon the door.

Enter, and persuade. Don't forget to say I'm a graduate, and don't forget the high office I'll hold."

So the go-between said "Yes," and entered the house, and Ah Woy, outside, heard voices in fierce argument, and he trembled for fear the marriage-maker might fail. I don't know why it should be, but proposals of marriage *do* weaken a man. There stood Ah Woy in the street, as strengthless as your mewyling little kitten, shaking and dreading a scornful "No."

By and by the go-between came forth. His eyes were still angry. "Her father is a man of stiff neck. Seldom have I been put to such wrangling. Let us drink sam shu for the dryness in my throat." "Yes. Yes. A drink. But, pah ngie, what . . . what of the marriage?" "Oh, the marriage? That will be next week." Oh, fortunate Ah Woy. Hold up your head. Pace like a tiger. . . . Married within the week.

Traveling on the river boat, down in Hiang Chwan, taking the journey to the town of his yamen, Ah Woy often said to his newly wedded wife, "I do not understand. When I saw you first, you were very tall. Now your stature is much decreased. And your other looks are not the same they were that day in the Street of The Dwellers in Happiness. You seem an entirely different person. But I am pleased and I would not change—not with the king—no, not for the lands of the king." This was on the river boat, slowly moved in Hiang Chwan.

Ah Woy had grown a longer name. He was now His Honor, The Magistrate, Wong (Ah) Woy Tsoo. A townsman, it was the carpenter, I think, appeared with despair on his face, and complaint on his tongue. "Honorable New Magistrate, my house has been entered by takers and stealers. The little silver I had is gone. Will you give me justice?" Wong Ah Woy spoke to his men. "All lictors, ma kuey (detective), go view the scene of horrid robbery. Take measurements; scrutinize boot tracks. Fetch the criminals to the house of the law."

The lictors went, but were slow to return. They brought no guilty man in chains. "A

hard case," they said. "It causes wrinkles in
our brows. The criminal left no name to
point suspicion." In the next day's search
they did no better. The third day closed
without an arrest. Wong Ah Woy, magistrate, grew uneasy. When justice is done,
the magistrate receives credit. When justice
falters, the magistrate receives blame. Many
a man has been removed from his yamen for
failure to detect a criminal. So Wong Ah
Woy slept fitfully at night. A dream repeated itself many times, without change.
This was the dream. "A piece of chalk in
jail."

Wong Ah Woy arose early and sent for
the carpenter. "Has a man named Chalk
a home in this town?"

"No, Sir. No."

"Mmmm. A man named Mark?"

"No. No. Not here."

"Mmmm. Chalk is white. Any Mr.
White?"

"Not in this village."

"Ahem. White is rice. Any Mr. Rice?"

"Oh, yes. Mr. Rice is my very good

friend. He wept most of all when he heard
of my loss."

Wong Ah Woy sent his lictors scurrying,
and so, Mr. Rice had cause to weep again.
He said he had stolen to pay a debt he owed
the carpenter. The money was secure under
his kitchen idol.

The new magistrate lost no sleep on his
next case. It was simplicity made easy. A
merchant complained. "I take oath to this.
The money was under my quilt. A very tall
man rolled me out of my bed. He grasped
the money, three bars, and ran. I could not
see his face, but I saw his height—very tall.
May I have justice?"

Wong Ah Woy instructed his lictors.
"Place hands on all very tall men. Six feet
of height is cause for suspicion. Go on horse-
back." (Hasten.)

The lictors knew their town thoroughly.
Soon they returned with the oilman, the
baker, several farmers, a thief, and the
mayor's grandfather, on his mother's side.
Wong Ah Woy said to the prisoners, "Speak

with straight tongues. Which tall man is
guilty of the stealing?"

They answered in a dozen voices, "Not I."

His Honor had prepared for a denial. "It
so happens I am friendly with a demon. He
offers to point me out the stealer. All men
enter yonder very dark room. In a little
while the demon will come and mark the
guilty man's back. The innocent backs will
not be marked." His prisoners entered the
darkened room. Wong Ah Woy called
loudly, an invitation to the demon. A lictor
made odd whistling noises. After a sufficient time, Wong Ah Woy opened the door.
"Come out," he said. "And *you* are the
thief. Thoroughly chalked on the back."

The oilman answered, "I am, it is true.
But I don't see how the Shen marked me. I
stood with my back tightly pressed to the
wall. How could he get behind me?"

His Honor might easily have explained
the mystery: "You foolish fellow, there was
no demon. I rubbed chalk upon the walls
of the very dark room. And you, thinking of

the guilt upon you, pressed your back to the wall." Howbeit, he said no such thing. He preferred to keep the secret.

Two women, dragging a little boy, entered His Honor's court. Together, they spoke; each pointing to each. "This terrible woman tried to steal my son. She claims the child is hers, but that is not true. Will Your Honor give me my son, and throw this depraved woman in jail?"

Wong Ah Woy took the child from them. He gazed at the small one's face, then at each of the women. He had hoped to detect a similarity. And of course, he failed. A baby looks like a baby, and nothing else; not like his grandpapa's uncle, Ching, as some people vow. The judge said, "Madam, is this *your* son? Stop biting my finger, you little villain."

The first woman answered, "It is. He's the very image of Wang Foo, his grandfather, the sweeper of Soo Lin Village."

His Honor turned to the other woman, "Madam, are you positive this is *your* son? Stop pulling my queue, you small imp." The second woman answered, "I am. He can say 'Da,' and another word, 'Wa,' and that's as much as Shih Chung (the great artist) could say when seventeen."

Thereupon the magistrate took chalk and drew a circle round the two where they stood on the floor. "Each woman is to grasp the child securely," said he. "Your strength seems to be equal. You, Mrs. Yang, are to pull. You, Mrs. Chu, are to pull. She who pulls the child out of this circle I shall recognize as the lawful mother." The first woman, Mrs. Yang, pulled with vigor. The second released her grasp. His Honor immediately wrote papers giving legal ownership to Mrs. Yang.

A friend, privileged to speak, remarked upon the case. "Your Honor, what is your reason for the decision just made?" Wong Ah Woy explained. "Ever since the day of the world's first judge the problem of awarding a child has been solved by a sword or a circle. The judge has always given the child to the woman who refused to see him torn in twain. Every book worth the price

The first woman, Mrs. Yang, pulled with vigor.

contains a story of the chalk circle. Now, today I had an extremely ignorant woman, and a woman well acquainted with the books. She had read of Shih Chung, who painted a picture of the Chalk Circle. Familiar with the circle, she expected me to follow the custom. But the other woman, a savage, would tear her child in pieces before giving him up. Nature is the rightest judge that ever quoted law. Besides . . . my wife told me which woman should have the child."

But evil pens were writing. The Chu family was far-spread and powerful. In the capital was a Chu, wearing chancellor's robes. "The magistrate Wong Ah Woy is not judicious," complained chancellor to king. "He sides with commoners, against the best families. Shall I not transfer him to Shan Cheen, where he can do less damage?"

"Wisest of all chancellors, yes," said the king. "Send him. There's even more oppression in Shan Cheen than Hiang Chwan would tolerate." So the order was written, and messengers ran by day and by night.

Wong Ah Woy packed his goods for travel.

With every stick and stitch he owned put in a box there was little more burden than a donkey could carry. But the law permitted free carriage of fifty piculs. The young magistrate knew that whether he journeyed with one picul or with fifty, the treasury would be made to pay for fifty, if not more. Then why not take advantage of an opportunity? His Honor began to scheme. As an aid to thinking he twirled the chalk upon his neck string. "Hao."

Forthwith Wong Ah Woy filled many boxes with merchandise.

His wife and his lark at his side, a caravan of baggage in trail, the magistrate went north to the capital city, to Chang An, city of the king.

But alas, or the sadder word, alack, don't think the chancellor considered his revenge complete. A Chu, a member of the famous Chu family, so often praised in story, had been made to lose face, by a mere upstart young magistrate. Well, the magistrate must suffer for his folly.

Spies watched upon Wong Ah Woy's

travel. They brought reports to Chang An that caused the chancellor to smile. But he didn't smile when he talked with the king. "My feelings are harrowed, Your Majesty. Bad news from Hiang Chwan. The magistrate Wong Ah Woy, I have reports, despoiled the people shamefully. He fined in every case, and every fine was every silver piece the prisoner owned. Camels, donkeys, whole farms he took. He accepted bribes, and headed a band of night thieves. He who went to Hiang Chwan with one plain coat for his back, now returns to Chang An with fifty cumbrous boxes."

"Dear. Dear," said the king. "Really so bad as that?"

"Quite," said the chancellor, out of his three-cornered mouth. "As an adviser to Your Majesty I *must* think the rogue Wong Ah Woy should be stripped of his forcibly gathered wealth."

"You've given worse advice than that," mused His Ruling Majesty. "As informer, you, of course, receive half of the magistrate's booty. The other half is needed in our treasury. Don't forget to summon me at the time you open the magistrate's baggage."

Wong Ah Woy pretended to a great surprise. His face was creased by lines of worry and dejection. "My miserable boxes really are not worth attention. They hold some few pieces of goods, so poor that I'd rather not have them displayed." "I'm quite ready to believe it," sneered Chancellor Chu. "Hammer them, and chisel them. Get the boxes open, men. We've caught a great thief this day." Workmen lifted hammers. The boxes burst wide and spilled their goods. . . . Out rolled uncountable pieces of chalk. Chalk. . . . Chalk. . . . And nothing else. The palace yard was whitened.

The chancellor, too, was whitened. He grew pale. But His Elevated Majesty, who ever had an eye for unusualities, all but came to smiling when he questioned Wong Ah Woy. "Most odd. Ahem. Young man, perhaps you'll explain what possessed you to assemble such little valued goods. Is our land of Hiang Chwan so poor?"

"Majesty," said Wong Ah Woy, "my

reasons are several. Suppose I had traveled light? The people who saw me must surely have said, 'Is Hiang Chwan so poverished that its magistrates have nought? I had intended to trade in that land, but now I shan't.' Hence, Your Majesty, our commerce would slacken. Bad times would come to the kingdom."

"Well reasoned," said His Majesty. "I hadn't thought of that."

"More to say," continued the magistrate, "the keepers of inns use great respect to a man of many boxes. To the poor man they show rudeness. I, though poor, traveled with extensive baggage, and the inn keepers were deceived thereby, and were respectful. In such manner I upheld the dignity of the magisterial robes."

"Well, and commendably done," vouchsafed the king. "When our ruling classes lose face, then trouble's in the making."

"Lastly," Wong Ah Woy went to the third of his reasons, "A magistrate should observe neatness. His queue should be tallowed, his robe unspotted, his boot soles be edged with whiting. Your Majesty, Sire, I've chalk enough to whiten my boots forever."

"A provident, a thoughtful young man," said the king, himself a stickler for neatness.

"Is our land of Hiang Chwan so poor?"

"A worthy young man, Chancellor, and extremely poor. Not a piece of money do I see in the boxes. Go to your money bags, Chancellor—don't snivel in my presence— and fetch some fine silver. Fill him a box, from your own large silver store. I'll not have this towardly young magistrate a pauper."

Happily I write it, Wong Ah Woy's career was far longer than the story tag to follow. Out in the west he gained his name, "Grandfather Guided by The Telltale Chalk." His children were beautiful, and his boots were always neatly whitened. Goodness knows he had plenty of chalk.

MING, THE MISER

MING, the miser, so they say, lived near Seang Tsoo. If that be true, he dwelt in a good region. The land is sweet, and gives sweetness. The people there raise barley, dolichos, melons, jujubes, turnips, and yellow potatoes. They have money. Even little boys may be seen with a penny.

Huey Tswok, carrying a string of copper cash, said to Ming, the miser, "How do I dare ask if you have eaten rice? You have, of course, and you smack your lips. Honorable Ming, the trees in your garden are hung with good blue plums. In this whole country no plums are like them. May I buy a full basket of your excellent plums?" Ming answered, "You have copper, in money form. I see it on your shoulder. Yes, I'll sell plums, but you must wait until I prepare the plums for selling."

Huey Tswok was in no hurry. "To be sure I can wait. No doubt it will take time to select the larger fruits for your steadfast old friend. And you wish to polish with a cloth each plum. That is good. It will make the fruit more attractive to the eye." But when Ming finally came with a basket, his plums showed no polish. Some of them seemed to have been gathered from a puddle of clay. (And, by the by, they weren't so large.) Huey Tswok commented. "Beautiful plums, yet, in a way, peculiar. Tell me, noble Ming, why has each plum a tiny hole in its side?" Ming replied, "You are a good neighbor, and keep your teeth together. (You do not talk.) Many people buy my plums in order to have the seeds for planting. They think to raise plums as good as mine, and sell them for less in the market. Ho. Ho. Ho. I laugh for each tree that never sprouts. The seeds can't grow. With my gimlet, I bore a hole through every seed."

The buyer shuffled his feet to leave, but Ming stopped him. "Wait, neighbor of over the way. For five more cash I'll carry the basket to your table. These plums are very heavy." He grasped the basket, so Huey Tswok had to shorten his cash rope by five.

Ming, the miser, always walked with long strides. He took one step where most men took two. By placing his feet less frequently upon the ground he saved boot leather. Carrying Huey Tswok's bought and paid for plums, the miser came to the wild Lan river. He made long jumps, to alight on every third stepping-stone. The basket threw him off balance. Down went Ming, in the worst of the stream, where the water roiled in swiftness. His son beheld the misfortune. The son exclaimed, "Honorable villagers, I cannot swim, and my father is drowning. Will no man wet his coat? I offer ten cash—ten cash—for the aid."

Old man Ming, swirling in the current, heard his son's shout. Perfectly furious, he screamed to the boy, "How dare you be so free with money? Five cash is enough. Offer five cash, of the smaller size." The villagers were reluctant. One said, "Those who travel by water should be prepared for a wetting. Ming won't drown. He'll come out with a handful of gold." Another said, "Quite true. And his sleeves will be filled with fish. He'll take advantage of the water if he possibly can." But Ming's screams of "Five cash only," were growing weaker. His son shouted "Eleven." The mayor, who was a kindhearted man, spoke to his people. "He is, is he not, our neighbor? Throw him a rope. Throw him an *old* rope, so there will be no great loss if he claims it for his own."

The cordage-maker heaved a rope. He, the mayor, the hammersmith, and the astrologer pulled handily. When Ming came close to shore, the tailor clutched him. It was neatly done. Ming had every right to say his

prettiest thanks. But, no. He scolded his
son. "You are so liberal, now you can go earn
the eleven cash that I told you not to offer.
Go work with your hands, or beg with your
tongue. You'll get no eleven cash from me."
To the men who had aided he spoke with still
more violence. "Look at my coat, you over-
strong rascals—no two threads are hanging
together. I'll take you to the magistrate's
court, sue the whole lot, for malicious rippage
of garments." His coat *was* torn, and no use
denying it. The tailor had pulled with un-
called-for vigor. Ming's weak coat had come
away from his back in handfuls.

Later, at the tailor's shop, Ming complained. "Some evil-hearted fellow tore my
coat as I climbed from the river. I wish I
knew the man. Were you there, and did you
see who tore my cloth?" The tailor trembled
slightly. "I sew coats, strongly. Let me
fashion a new one. Only fifty cash." "Fifty
cash," howled Ming. He said it was out-
rageous, hinting that all robbers were not
upon the king's high road. Finally, the tailor
reduced his price. "Forty cash." "Very

well," said Ming, "but I brought the cloth with me. You must take off twenty cash for that. I also brought thread; there's ten cash saved. And here are my scissors for you to use; that's five cash saved."

The befuddled tailor was compelled to make Ming's coat for nothing—and pay five cash for the privilege.

Ming was still very wet from his douse in the river. The day was cloudy, so he couldn't stand in the sun to dry. He had to go home. But he wouldn't burn his expensive wood. He searched for straws upon the road side. With weeds and straws the miser built a little fire. A neighbor's cat came in to enjoy a warming. "I've no free fire for beggars' cats. Get out," screamed Ming. In stretching for the cat he kicked fire upon the rush covered floor. The straw bed flamed. The thatched roof caught sparks. Ming's house soon lighted the village.

Came the hammersmith, the mayor, the leatherman, the candler, others, all came. A stranger stood in the front of the crowd, saying "Ohs" and "Ahs." "How now?"

shrieked Ming the miser. "You come uninvited to see my house burn? Pay me five cash for what you have seen." "But, honored Sir, I thought it was free. I am a stranger in this part of the world, and don't know the customs. When I saw that your house had encountered the fire demons I came to offer assistance. I expected to make no charge, and certainly not to be charged." "Pay me five cash, or be dragged by the magistrate's lictors to jail." The stranger had to yield. "Be it so. But I have no money with me. You'll have to go to my house, in Kwong Shing Village, and get it there."

Ming was so eager to secure his money that he soon started toward Kwong Shing Village. With his long strides he went swiftly. A man came by on a beast of riding. "Why pull myself, when I can be pulled?" reasoned Ming the miser. He grasped a saddle leather, and the donkey hauled him to town. "I'll save my breath, if nothing more. And anything saved is as good as something earned." But the riding man was so frightened he screamed all the way.

Next day, servants of the king appeared in the village. They carried their tablets; they had chains and bamboos. The captain commanding said, "This is a very bad village. It harbors a scamp. Last night, as the king's emissary galloped the village street, some ill-conditioned person tried to steal his donkey. A villager grasped the emissary's donkey from behind and tried to pull it away. Do you know the would-be thief?" "It must have been some other village," suggested the mayor. "We have no such terrible person with us. For my part, I already have a donkey, and shouldn't care for another." The captain commanding put emphasis upon his words. "*This*, and not another, is the guilty village. We have come to punish a man for attempted donkey-theft. If you won't produce him, you must draw lots. The astrologer has straws. Draw. He who selects the short straw shall know the king's wrath."

The hammersmith drew. The money changer drew. Then the tinker. Then the doctor. Next in line was Ming. In his greed the old fellow clutched a handful of straws.

His nature was too strong for his well-being. The king's captain opened Ming's hand. "The short straw." "The short straw," echoed the mayor. He smiled. But do not think he smiled at Ming's misfortune. The mayor was a just man. And his turn to draw would have been next.

Now, Ming the miser was woefully ailing. What with a fever from his flogging, and a chill got from the river, he lay at death's door. The neighbors did what they could. They pounded drums and set off fire-crackers. But the demon of sickness remained with poor Ming. The demon refused to be frightened by noise, and there was no medicine to drive him.

The carpenter went to the doctor. He had been under a strain. His eyes were moist, and his voice was unsteady. "Doctor, please save our old friend Ming. Pull him back from the grave. Ming wishes me to sell him an expensive nan wood coffin, for practically nothing. His persuasion is great, and I fear I will yield. Send him the surest, unpleasantest medicine, doctor. I will pay for it.

Cure him. Then he won't need a coffin."
The doctor promised to do his best, as soon
as he could find time. Meanwhile, he would
send his brother-in-law, a beggar and doing
well, with a tube of the most startling prep-
arations.

Ming swallowed the medicine and laughed
as he felt the demon of sickness leaving his
body. The neighbors pounded kettles with
renewed vigor. The doctor's beggar-in-law
brother stood near by. He said to Ming, "Is
there something you wish to give me? I had
a long and hasty walk. Copper is good for
rubbing tired muscles." Ming replied, "*I* am
the one whose palm should be coppered. You
have much and should give. When the neighbors hear that I have swallowed your medicine they will think it good, and so will buy
whole gallons." The beggar's opinion was
thoroughly different, at first. But in the end,
he weakened. "It is all, everything I have.
This gourd for begging is all. But you shall
have. Take my gourd, with a welcome in it.
And as soon as you are better, I'll pay you
well—to teach me my trade."

The gourd wouldn't serve for ladling

broth. It leaked and wasted. Ming hung it on a pagoda-tree at the village well. The wind blew upon Ming's begging-gourd and made sweet music. The gourd gave a music like harps-and-flutes. A traveler paused at the well and stood with a listening look. Ming said, "You must pay me for my music." The traveler replied, "Speak louder. I am deaf." In fury, Ming seized (I wish that word were easier to spell) his gourd and raised it to throw. The traveler exclaimed, "Stop. Don't break it. It is pretty, and I will buy it. Here, honorable musician, accept this book—I am only a miserable scholar —and let me have the gourd."

Ming thought he had made a good bargain. He didn't know the way of books, with their little print, requiring so much light. That night, in his dark house, the miser said to himself, "My book is doing me no good what-sover. I can't even see its shape. The printer should have furnished it with candles. What a shame is here; I have a book, and can't read it for darkness." Once he fumbled for a candle, but soon thought better.

The king, with vast train of men and

beasts, was encamped in the market square. He had a fine fire blazing. The story-teller was reciting a yarn of amazing olden times. "So Prince Chang, with no man to aid him, rode into the thick of forty thousand foes, and hewed them to the earth." A villager walked into the flame-lighted circle, and sat on his heels, elbows nearly in the fire. He opened a book, and from it read in a sing-song whine. "The courtiers addressed him, saying, 'There is a youth in a low station, called Yu Shu.' His Majesty said, 'Oh yes. Good. I have heard of him. But how are his qualities?' The guardian of the four emi-nences said, 'He is a blind man's son. His father is evilly crazy. . . .'"

Said the king to the mayor, 'A bold man you have in this village. What is his name? How are his qualities? Has he an iron neck?" The mayor answered, "He, Your Majesty, goes by the name Ming, Ming the miser." He told of Ming's great love for money, exaggerating, of course, to gain a heartier laugh at the end of his story. But when he had done he heard no royal merriment. The king sat silent behind his beard and thoughtfully gazed at the one so cruelly slandered.

"I'll clap him in jail," said the mayor. "Too stingy to burn his own candles, he takes light from Your Majesty's fire." "Do nothing so silly and wrong," said the monarch. "It comes upon me I can use a man of saving talent. If he can lock my treasury door, and keep it locked against all pleadings, then he's a man I've long been wanting. I shall make him head of my wealth department."

High office made no change in Ming. He couldn't change. The king had forbidden. The king had said, "You are my treasurer now. Apply the rules you have learned so well. Save. Save. And again, Save. Turn the key, and say 'No' the whole day through."

Soldiers came to the treasury door. They came with their palms turned up, to receive. They wanted money. But let them speak for it. "Please, Honorable Treasurer Ming, we are back from the war, and haven't a copper between us. We fought like dragon sons, like demons crossed in love, and now we

should like our pay." Ming rebuffed them.
"You are so strong in the fight, go fight again,
and take your wages from the enemy."

The Minister for Defence of The Realm
came to Ming with a wheedling story. "Our
western wall is flat on the ground. There's
nothing to hinder a foe in the west. Give
me money to buy quarry-stone and build an
unclimbable wall." Ming hooted at the
thought. "Extravagance and Ruin. Not a
keg of gold will I open for such hoddy-
doddy prodigence. Esteemed Defence Man
please learn that quarry-stone is highly expensive."

But Ming knew very well that the wall
must be built, for the times were like now,
distressingly unsettled. He went to the
Commissioner of Fortifications. "I see many
bricks piled up in the east. Send laborers
to tear them down, and erect them again in
a high western wall. But hire cheap men,
and whip them at work, else I'll pay no
money for the building."

The General Commanding The Cavalry
Corps foolishly asked for a favor. "Our

"You are so strong in the fight, go fight again and take your wages from the enemy."

cavalry donkeys are going unfed. They need beans and hay and long-fodder. Give me money before they starve." The king's vigilant treasurer answered. "Is it likely I'd be such a wastethrift? Your cavalry cattle do nothing but eat, and carry captains around the town to make the social calls. I shall hire out every donkey to a miller to turn his mill. Then money will come to the treasury, instead of going out."

Ming had many arguments, but he also had his way. The king was behind him with "Perfectly right." When bills came in for the western wall construction, Ming wept and roared. "Money they want, in tremendous weights. So be it, the thieves. I'll give them money by tons." He ordered the founders to mold iron money, and paid all bills with iron. But when tax days came and mandarins rode in to pay, Ming told them, "Gold and silver, please."

An enemy crossed the border and moved on rapid feet to take the capital city. The royal army broke out its flags and stood in the path of invasion. Strong guns boomed

to turn the foemen. His Majesty waited
with a smile to receive good news from the
field. Soon a general came limping in, weary
and woebegone. "We've lost the fight, Sire.
We're whipped, and no fault of ours. Where
is that honorable imbecile treasurer? He
hired out our war-donkeys to work in mills,
and that is why we lost. The donkeys went
round and round in circles, just as they had
learned while turning millstones. They tram-
pled our own foot-soldiers deep in the dust
and the enemy tramped them still deeper."

In rushed another high servant. He was
utterly out of breath, and the title he bore
was Minister For Defence of The Realm.
"Majesty, your honorable idiot treasurer will
surely cost us the war. He built us a wall
in the west—and where did he get the bricks?
From the east, Majesty. He tore down the
eastern wall to build a wall in the west. . . .
And the enemy is marching on our unpro-
tected east."

The king, with a duty to be done, presently sought his honorable treasurer. Rather
sadly, yet not so sadly either, he let his serv-

ant go. "You saved, as I told you, Ming, but not, I fear, quite wisely. The officers clamor for a new treasurer . . . and I grieve to say it, your head. Take your coat from the peg and go away. The assistant will pay you what salary is due. Pay him, Treasurer-Assistant . . . in iron money."

Ming the miser, going home, loaded his iron upon a cart. He reached Lan Ssu Kwat, and all was well. But climbing the rocky hill near Lo Shan Temple his cart broke down. No one would pay for repairs. . . .

They say you can still see Ming's iron money on the roadside.

THE SHEN WHO MISUNDERSTOOD

WENG FOO was an artist, very proud of the pictures he painted, but more proud by thrice of his little daughter, Oo Kiao. Oo Kiao, that's an astonishing name. It means "Ugly Little Person." The reason for such a terrible name is this. Name a girl "Perfectly Beautiful," and the demons, so persistently alert, will talk as I have it here. "Perfectly Beautiful, say you so? That's ung tou (worth hearing). *Perfectly Beautiful*—WE'LL TAKE HER." For the demons act upon what they *hear*. Therefore, a girl is called "Ugly Little Person," and the demons frowningly exclaim, "Let's be gone. She is ugly—Ugly Little Person. Let's leave her at home."

Weng Foo and his pretty little daughter, named Ugly Little Person, strolled down the caravan road, to put the scenes of springtime on their tablets. Weng Foo beheld a sheep nibbling grasses upon a rounded hillock, and he murmured, "It is beautiful. I feel that this will be my finest picture. Let me have the brushes, daughter, and do get me a cup of water. I must hurry, to finish my work while in the proper mood." Oo Kiao meaningfully held the brushes behind her. She took not even a first step toward the pebbly stream. Instead, she said, "Why it's only a sheep with a twisted horn. Sheep are very nice, but they have no color. Besides, Daddy, we have painted a thousand sheep already. Let's follow the road and have an adventure.'

What could Weng Foo do? Nothing. He had to bid the finest sheep farewell. He and Oo Kiao rambled down the caravan road. At every turn, and turns are many, Oo Kiao expected to find a golden dragon or a fiery phoenix. But the scenes were humdrum and every-dayish. Finally Oo Kiao decided, "I am tired. I think I shall play with some daisies—although they are merely white." Weng Foo was suited exactly. He said, "No one could have chosen better. You play with the daisies, and I'll do likewise, upon paper. This is an attractive setting."

So the artist dabbled his brushes and began to paint the things he saw, or wanted. He didn't want the many travelers in his picture, because they were dusty shouting fellows, and were without beauty. But the travelers, every last man Wang, Lang, and Sang, of them, stopped to gaze upon the fir-flower tablet and its colored marks. All made comments to indicate that they liked, or thought little, or thoroughly disapproved. A tea coolie of nice appreciation said, "See. He puts the scene upon paper. Magnificent." And a companion spoke up with a "So he does. So it is. Ho. Ho. 'It's pretty,' as the monkey said when he dipped his paw in the indigo vat." Another wayfarer on a donkey declared, "Well painted. Charming.

He will receive much money for that." But the man behind him asked simply, "Why?"

As it turned out, Oo Kiao came to be the severest critic on the road that day. It was really the artist's own fault. He imagined he had painted something far above the ordinary. He stood away from his picture and gazed at it admiringly, holding his hands in congratulation and drawing in his breath, as people do when well satisfied. Of course he talked. "Now I may call myself an artist. Shen Hao. There is the tree with fish-scale bark, just as the masters paint. All branches are shown upon the left side—quite proper. The clouds are absolutely round—what could be more artistic? Daughter, look at my picture, and tell me what thoughts you have." Oo Kiao said, "I don't like it. Earth-brown, and wishy-washy blue, and weak green aren't pretty colors. I like dragon-blood red, and plum-side purple, and indigo, and strong yellow." The astonished Weng Foo murmured, "Well. Well. Well," and he wasn't well pleased. However, he was a man, and so he couldn't admit he might be mistaken. "Well.

"Now I may call myself an artist."

Well. Well. Yellow, red, and purple," he
muttered. "Just for fun, I shall use all those
colors, and more. Then you'll see how hideous a picture can be."

Weng Foo had been teaching his daughter
how to paint. He thought he now had an
excellent opportunity to teach the small critic
how *not* to paint. He made a long streak of
indigo. The reddest red he had was put on
just above. Slashes of orange color followed
the red. Purple came next; he splashed it on
higgledy-piggledy. Patches of pink and
blobs of green were used in the little space
remaining. Weng Foo moralized learnedly.
"Now, my dear, you see? It looks like a
ram's-horn wind in a colorman's shop. Let
this be a lesson to you."

A foot-traveler had paused to view the picture. This man was an ancient. He appeared to have lived through his first thousand years, and to be well begun on his second. He grinned extensively, gazing first at
the picture, then at the cliffs and the sky.
Weng Foo felt much ashamed. He threw a
cloth over his picture. The ancient one was

not offended; he added chuckles to his grin.
From his girdle he took a well-filled purse.
"Ah," said he. "I thrill to that. Shen Hao.
Brother, I have a seeing eye, but never I saw
the like of that. Will you sell? This is the
real gold. I dig it from San•Kwa Mountain
when ever I have need. Ho. Ho. Ho.
You may have the whole pouch for that
picture."

Weng Foo had an honesty of more than
mere so-so, average quality. He saw at once
that the old man was an ignorant country
fellow, perhaps crazy into the bargain. He
scorned to take advantage of such simplicity.
"I could never be guilty of selling this atrocious daub. It is impossible. I mean to destroy it at once." (The old man seemed
ready to weep.) "But," continued Weng
Foo, "if you really care so much—though I
can't see why—I'll give it to you. Only, I
pray you, never tell anyone that *Shih Huen*
painted it." Shih Huen. Mmmmm. Had
he lost memory of his own name?

The aged person smiled and smirked his
happiest. "Honorable Shih Huen, I am

grateful. I give thanks now, and another day I shall double them. You and I have similar tastes. Eat plenty of rice." Weng Foo said, "Walk slowly."

As the queer person went his road he carefully dropped some coins where he knew Oo Kiao would find them. All in all, a very decent man.

Weng Foo painted another picture; this time in the proper school manner. He liked it well, but held his tongue from boasting. Evening time shadows were creeping bluely from the hills. The painter and his daughter strolled toward their distant home. They had many ups to climb, and deep ravines to saunter through. At a place where the road went down and down, and the cliffs rose high on either side, Oo Kiao paused to make a remark. "Look, Daddy. See the pretty colors." Weng Foo rubbed his eyes. He said, "Surely I am still seeing that terrible picture I gave to the wanderer. These cliffs have always been the color of plain stone and common earth. Now, I seem to see them red, and blue, and violet confused. But that can't be. I fear my eyes are stricken, Daughter. Pink, green, foxy, yellow—oh, my eyes." Oo Kiao dissented, "Your eyes are not stricken, One-with-the-stick (daddy). The cliffs have been colored just like the picture you painted and said so ugly, and I liked best of all. I think the nice old person with the gold must be a man-witch." But Weng Foo would not have it that way. "You are dreaming, Daughter, and my poor old eyes have been hurt by the picture. Ai Yu. Take my hand, little Oo Kiao, and lead me home." So Oo Kiao took her father's hand, and guided him through donkey trains and camel droves, up from the traveled road to the quiet woodland path. Weng Foo stumbled often. The man could see perfectly well. Yet he was so positive he could not, that no doubt he really couldn't.

The artist always insisted upon sleeping-mouse-like stillness in his studio. On Oo Kiao's noisy days her father never let her enter his work room. He said and pretended that he must hear the slap of his brush, else he couldn't know how the colors were flowing.

He was painting a sheep from memory when something thwacked the door. "Thwack." It was a very loud thwack, unexpected and startling. The artist upset a pot of red. He said, crossly. "Go away, Oo Kiao. Or, if it is Chi Chin, go away." Chi Chin (Famine), was Oo Kiao's little dog.

The door opened, and in stepped the old man of the day before. Weng Foo's face was dour, but the old man's beamed pleasure. "Pleasant rice and fat red herring is my wish to you, honorable Shih Huen. I found you only after much talk and several blows. The foolish and deceptive villagers, your neighbors, vowed they had never heard of a man named Shih Huen. But when they said Mr. Weng was the only painter here around, I knew they were merely ignorant of your flowery name. I brought gold, and expect to carry away pictures. Will you sell?"

"Willingly. Select those you like, and I'll name reasonable prices. This, Study of A Grey Goose Feather, is my best painting. Put the spectacles upon your nose and see." The old man looked, and shook his head. He looked at other pictures, looked at all of them, and continued to shake. Finally he said, "Evidently I am mistaken. In the face you quite resemble Shih Huen, but in the paint there is no kinship between you two."

Weng Foo was trying to explain when the visitor saw the pot of red upset upon a paper. A shriek of joy announced the discovery. "Oh yes, you are, you *are* Shih Huen, you are. Ho. Ho. Here is the picture I want; the best I've seen in a wandering long life." Weng Foo said, "But. . . . Honorable stranger. . . . You misunderstand. . . ." The picture was only a blot. Weng Foo meant to enlighten his visitor.

The old man thought it a refusal. "Really, you *must* let me have this. Perhaps you do not understand. I am a Shen. I am the Shen of Passion and beauty. . . . The world is too drab—too drear. I want to make changes for the brighter all around. Consider the flowers. They have many shapes, but only one shade—white, plain white. It is monotonous. Now, this red picture, which you are to sell me, I shall use in coloring a flower, the hibiscus. . . . Let us make a bargain, Shih Huen. Be my picturer of flowers. All you've to do is draw flowers and paint them in plenty of color. I promise you shall wear tribute silks, and your kettle will always know the feel of rice." Weng Foo was so dazed that he accepted the Shen's offer.

The artist drew roses and colored them yellow. More roses, and made them pink. Lilies he made, red and golden. He drew the paulownia blossom-bells and colored them purple. Pansies—you know what they are— pied. Once he forgot and drew another sheep. Weng Foo was fond of sheep. He colored it red. But the Shen never saw it. Otherwise, today we'd have red sheep upon our hills, and perhaps our coats would be tomato color.

The Shen came often. Always he brought a pouch of coins: he had absolutely no idea of the value of gold. Each time he carried away a few more pictures. And the fields and gardens changed from green and white, to all other colors and green.

Oo Kiao had long been learning to paint.

Upon her fir-flower tablet she made many a quaint and unknown figure. The greatest trouble was a quick impatience. Sometimes the brush grew stubborn and refused to set down lines to Oo Kiao's liking. When that happened she merely threw the brush away and used her finger to lay on paint.

One day when the brush was unusually ill-willed, the little girl tried a new plan. She dipped three fingers into the color pot, then dabbed them against her tablet. The result was something like a rabbit track, turned purple. Oo Kiao admired the mark. She made a number of three-daub purple rabbit tracks. Her father had been idly gazing through the moon-window. He said, "Daughter, I am displeased with my work today. I shall give over the painting until I feel more up to it. Perhaps a walk will start new ideas. You keep house, and if anyone asks for me, turn your face toward the pine forest and call." Oo Kiao promised. And she really meant to obey. Now and then she practised calling, and practised talking to an imaginary visitor, quite haughtily.

"Thwack." In came the door, and in came
the Shen. "Where is the paper?" said the
Shen. He saw a paper in Oo Kiao's hand,
and promptly took it. Oo Kiao was too
scared to hold it back. The Shen grinned
mightily. "Ah," said he. "Now the man is
painting to my taste. Look at the color.
This is, *decidedly* is, the very best thing he
has done." Oo Kiao tried to explain. "But.
. . . Mr. Shen. . . . Father is down in the
pines, and he left word. . . ." "I know. I
know," said the Shen. "Left word to take
what I like. Tell him I left the gold on the
table. I'm in a hurry today. Eat plenty of
rice and rose candy." He rushed away with
Oo Kiao's paperful of purple little rabbit
tracks.

Of course, the Shen misunderstood. He
thought he had bought Weng Foo's painting
of a wonderful new flower. Soon the woods
were thousand-filled with little flowers, tzu
loh lan, which we have learned to call
"violets." But the wonderful painting was
merely Oo Kiao's paper of three-finger marks

The Shen came to Weng Foo's house and

Oo Kiao was too scared to hold it back.

told him of a scheme. "I have in mind, brother artist, a sign to be put in the sky. I want a sign that will assure all men it isn't going to rain any more. This morning we had a thunder storm. It was soon past and done with. Yet, whole cities of men remained in their houses, under their beds, all day, fearing the rain was not finished. Paint me, perhaps, a brilliant crimson tree to place in the sky after finished rain." Weng Foo said, "I'll gladly paint such a sign, esteemed Shen. Many times I have wished to go strolling, yet feared to go, because I thought the rain not ended. A crimson tree, then. Shall I have fruit upon it?" The Shen laughed. "Yes. Let the tree bear fruit. Then after every storm I'll shake apples down on the people. If they don't see the sign, they'll certainly feel it."

Weng Foo put his heart and plenty of color into his work. He painted a crimson tree in the most approved ancient-master style. He placed all branches on the left side. He placed the required three knots on the bole. But he was not pleased with the

picture. Nor did he think the Shen would
be pleased. Thinking so, he painted another
tree, this one orange—not an orange tree, but
an orange color. When he had finished he
said, "Pu hao. Kai tan." You will see,
then, that Weng Foo was not pleased.

Meanwhile Oo Kiao was no less busy than
her famous father. Oo Kiao painted upon a
large sheet of paper the most capital of capital O's, done in red. Inside the red capital
O she painted an orange O. Inside that she
put a yellow one. No, not a one at all, but
another O. Then came green, blue, indigo,
and that very nice color, violet.

And then Oo Kiao's little Chi Chin, the
little dog so spoiled, who had been longing
for a chance, seized the paper of many O's
and tore it utterly in two. Oo Kiao really
was compelled to say what she said. She
said "O." And with severity, "You've destroyed a masterpiece—and the paint may be
bad for you. Come here." But the puppy
barked, and kept at a distance. He ate his
half of the paper.

Weng Foo had painted many trees, all

Chi Chin seized the paper of many O's and tore it utterly in two.

thoroughly unlovely. He was quite ready to be provoked. He grumbled, "Oo Kiao, no noise. No noise, Chi Chin. Come, Daughter give me your paints. Give me the papers Now, you and Chi Chin go into the garden for a romp." He placed the paints upon the top side of a shelf. The paper he put into an out-of-reach drawer.

While Oo Kiao persuaded Chi Chin to come from beneath the table, her father changed his mind. Weng Foo said, "Wait. I have decided otherwise. You, Oo Kiao, stay here and keep house, while I stroll amid the pines and study. Stay here, Oo Kiao, and paint your doll-children red." His daughter promised—though she secretly decided upon purple, not red. Weng Foo handed down brushes and colors, but forgot the paper. Away he went to the forest of pines, where ideas may be caught as they fly.

The little Chi Chin's hair stood up in hairbrush straightness. He barked his most savage "don't come near." Oo Kiao knew that a visitor must be approaching. She was not even slightly startled when a walking stick thwacked against the door. In came the Shen. "I hope you are not hungry," said the Shen. "I hope the same thing for your barking dog. Where did your father put the paper?" The little girl answered with her prettiest "Thank you, Mr. Shen, we have eaten. Chi Chin, let loose of Mr. Shen's cloth coat. My daddy's papers are in the

high-up drawer, but he doesn't like them."
The Shen gave the drawer a pull. His face
showed pleased surprise. He said, "Your
father changed his mind, didn't he?" The
Shen was thinking of the crimson tree he had
discussed with Weng Foo. But Oo Kiao was
thinking how her father had told her, first,
to play in the garden, then, to stay in the
room. She replied, "Yes, Mr. Shen, he
changed his mind, and now he's gone to study
and stroll." The Shen declared, "I'm glad
he did change. I think this picture, I'll vow
I do, is exactly what I've been wanting.
Here's the bag of gold upon the table. Eat
plenty of rose candy." He shook off Chi
Chin, and closed the door behind him.

And again the Shen had misunderstood.
He had taken Oo Kiao's half of an O, instead
of her father's correctly painted tree.

That very noon the world went in hiding
from a terrible storm. There was wind to
drive the rain swiftly, and giant's-organ
thunder, and lightning to spell sharp Z's
upon the clouds. Then the sun came out,
and all men beheld a painted, huge half-

circle in the sky. And they all admired it, saying, "Beautiful. That is the Shen's sign for no more rain. Now we can go to the market square and talk. We can feel assured our coats will come home dry."

It is true that Weng Foo, famous artist, painted rose, and hibiscus, and pansy for the Shen. But please remember this. Oo Kiao painted violets. Oo Kiao painted the half-O rainbow. . . . And Chi Chin ate the other half.

FAR TO VOYAGE

HE was a person of youth, of handsomeness, and high desire. I speak of Ching.

Kwan Ching, having studied his hundred books, sat in Learning's Hall to take the examination. He graduated, and good for him. He received the Complete Scholar degree. What he did *not* receive was the appointment to be governor of Kiang Sing. And he had counted on that. His honorable parents had sent a gift of gold, in various bright shapes, to the chancellor, sent it because they admired the chancellor, though they had never seen that elevated man, and not at all as a reminder that their son desired to be governor of Kiang Sing.

But alas, the times were changing. An empress, Her Majesty Yot Yuh Feen (bow the head, all men), graced the throne and ruled the land. This lady, though undoubtedly beautiful, and quite pleasing in most respects, unfortunately was mis-gifted with a great curiosity. She made inquiries concerning the chancellor, and the treasurer, various governors, magistrates, and the comptroller of the four eminences. When she learned the truth, whatever it was, she called for letters of resignation from these men, and appointed women to many of the very highest offices.

For the first time ever, a woman governor sat in Kiang Sing. Kwan Ching, and this is no exaggeration, was dumfounded. He was indeed, nonplussed. Kwan Ching grieved, "Talent is no longer respected in this topsy-turvy realm. Yesterday I graduated, with every expectation of being governor tomorrow, and wealthy the next day. I who can recite the entire Book of Changes, backward and without error, am to hold no privileged rank. Under the empress there's no justice in the land. I shall shake its dust from my boots, or if the day be rainy, I'll shake its clinging clay. I shall go beyond the back lands of the empire, or north, or south, or eastward in a ship." And this grievous speech had barely quit his lips when an uncle, his name Kwan Tok, approached and said, "Tomorrow, my sailing-ship parts the waters southward. I go upon the ocean, far to voyage. To the Moluccas for spices, to Yang Seang for sandalwood, or to Foo Yat Sun for apes, whatever way the wind blows. And my ship sails at tide rise. You, my brother's son, may share, if you will, the admiral's cabin. Come with me, and see stranger sights than those made green and red in pictured books."

To the invitation, Kwan Ching replied quite as one could wish. "I thank my honored father's elder gracious brother. At the time of putting to sea I shall be in board.

There is no justice between the borders of this land. I shall seek a country where righteousness flourishes, and talent has its reward. In the Moluccas, or Yang Seang, or in Foo Yat Sun, perhaps I shall find contentment and advance."

But, as I, the kiang kou yin (teller of old tales), shall endeavor hereinafter to make clear, Kwan Ching was not to visit these mentioned countries. Sailed and sailed the ship, out of cold water into warm. Serpents of the sea grudgingly made room for passage. Leviathan swam hungrily in the wake. Dragons betwixt sun and sea, cast shadows fearsome to the mariners. With clouds the wind arose, and gained, and was a storm. Storm increased and was a gale. To hurricane the gale changed, and where it moved, the rigging shrieked, and the spars snapped, and blackness lay upon the waters.

The frightened sailors turned to and gave their idols a threshing, but Kwan Ching and Kwan Tok tied themselves to beams of buoyant lightwood. Their ship, they knew, was losing strength. A time would come for the

planking to open like my lady's fan. The
sea, too, knew this thing. It threw its waves
to the top of the mast. And the winds increased, and the waters struck with heavier
force . . . and broken timbers washed upon
the shore.

They upon the land, the dwellers there,
expressed much sorrow. One who by his
robes, was mayor, spoke officially the city's
vast regret. "Our heads are low in shame
that such misfortune should overwhelm our
guests. It is entirely our fault. We knew
the coast to be rocky, yet nothing did to
make it smooth. But we shall do such resti-
tution as we can. Searchers are now bringing
in your trade goods. A house has been set
apart for your comfort. Walk where you
please in our city. No locks are here, but
only open doors."

Kwan Tok, who chanced to be somewhat
older than his nephew, had the right to answer the mayor's civility. "Your words are
like a melon—sweet. It is a great pleasure
to be seawrecked, and be swept to a land of
such rare hospitality. We accept your kind-

ness, with protestations of never-to-lessen gratitude."

Various citizens appeared with sandals,

hey upon the land, the dwellers there, expressed much sorrow.

nd soups, and suits in their arms. They resented their gifts to the sea-beaten visi- ors, and discreetly retired.

Dry clothing and slumbered rest soon worked for complete recovery. While they ate their way through a king's own dinner, Kwan Tok declared, "This is a remarkable country. Instead of robbing us—and I have been wrecked ten times, and robbed twice that—these people bestow kindness. Remarkable, indeed." Kwan Ching said, "Where you speak remarkable twice, I am minded to use the word till breathless. This is truly a remarkable land. The clothing given us has never had a man in it—clean and new. The girdle pouches bulge with gold. And we, to these people, are only foreigners." Kwan Tok said, "True. Yes. Undoubtedly. Remarkable." His words were well spaced, for the slugs-in-paste lured him to give up the conversation.

After so long a time the younger one suggested, "Now that we are dry-skinned and well-dinnered, let us walk in a street and observe the ways of the people." Kwan Tok replied, "Good to do. Let us walk, and thereby coax the sea-staggers out of our legs. This, I take it, is a door; made to function like the doors at home. But observe the sign upon it. 'Ghosts invited to enter and refresh themselves.' Remind me, Ching, to ask at a shop for ink. I'll write before we go to bed."

The shopkeeper was deep in an argument with a customer. Their talk was loud. A man who thinks himself cheated is hardly likely to whisper. Kwan Ching and Uncle Kwan Tok listened to talk seldom heard in lands this side of the weak Jo Shuey waters. "The goods is third grade, and third only by courtesy. Sleazy and worthless, it won't last a wearing from now to next day. Oh, how utterly bad it is." And that . . . was the merchant speaking. I'll say it twice . . . the merchant speaking. The seller, not the buyer.

When the customer spoke, as he did with a rush, it was to sound a strong denial. "Not so, though I beg pardon for my rudeness. We two, it seems, cannot see eye and eye together. This goods is strong as tent cloth. The roses on it raise its value greatly. I hold to my first offer. 500 cash, and I'm to do the counting." The merchant laughed un-

pleasantly. "You carry a joke too far, honorable customer. 200 cash is my price. As
to counting our law gives me that privilege. 200 is my last word." Th

"250 cash," said the merchant.

customer seemed to realize that he had been a trifle unreasonable. He said, in a tone of compromise, "Let's squabble no more. Accept 450 cash and say you hold no enmity against me."

"250 cash," said the merchant, with hi chin well up. "250, once and for all." Th customer walked to the door, and a step be

yond. That was done as a threat. He
thought to scare the dealer into acceptance.
When the plan failed, he turned and said,
"I admit I am outwitted. Here are cash to
the number of 400. Please fold the goods in
a paper." Instead the merchant placed his
goods upon a shelf. "It is foolish to attempt
a deal with you, honorable customer. You
won't even offer so little as 300 cash. I am
stubborn, it is true, but right is right, and
cheating's wrong. The goods is worse than
thought. Pardon me now. I have other
customers to wait upon. Go to another shop,
and see how you fare." He seemed utterly
in earnest. The set of his face plainly
showed that he had made his last concession.

To work up a sympathy was the customer's
next scheme. "Surely you won't turn me
away, to be bullied and tricked by the heart-
less ones in other shops. Have pity on me,
gracious merchant. I am far too rich, *too*
rich. I am weakened by the heavy weight of
gold I carry. Be merciful, at 350 cash." He
pulled such a sad mouth, whined so piteously
that the man of the shop relented. "Very

well then. 350 let it be. But I measure,
with my own yardstick, and what's more important, *I* count the coins."

Now, the average person, which I hope no
one is, might think the argument had gone
far enough. But no indeed, not by five, ten,
minutes. The merchant measured, and craftily cut his silk a good two yards beyond the
end of his stick. The customer instantly
sensed a cheat. He screamed his objection.
"Oh, no, you overly-generous merchant. I
saw you go beyond the end. And look at this
measuring stick, twice the legal length, and
I dare say easy to stretch. I asked for five,
and you give me ten." He sheared the goods
in two.

When he offered his money he received
more cause for dispute. The merchant pretended a lack of sight. "My eyes, as you
have seen, are giving me poor service today.
They can't tell san from sze. Tomorrow I'll
send my son to your house for the money."
The customer smiled grimly. "A scholar's
name for tomorrow is 'when the Yellow
River runs clear' (never). You are clever,

respected merchant, but you'll not take advantage of me in that way. I have had experience. Last week, a man to whom I owed money died. I at once brought suit against his widow, to compel acceptance of payment. Law is a vile thing, as we have it. The magistrate permitted me to pay only half of the money in which I stood indebted. I had no witnesses to prove I owed more. I'll never again be caught at such a disadvantage. Take the money, here and now."

Reluctantly, the merchant began to count. "Yih, urh, three, six, seven, nine, twelve." Many of the coins he selected were false, made of colored glue. All were small. He wouldn't touch the larger, more valuable cash.

At last the transaction was completed, to the full dissatisfaction of buyer and seller. Kwan Tok stepped forward. He selected a cake of ink, tested it for hardness and taste, found it first chop, and paid down ten cash, the usual price for ink of that quality and size. The merchant laughed heartily. "I am overjoyed to see our shipwrecked visitor has

recovered to such extent that he feels inclined
to jest. Ten cash, of course, is out of all
reason." Uncle Tok reddened. "Pardon me,
I am a stranger, and not familiar with prices
here. What do you ask? Fifteen?" The
merchant howled with glee. "Fifteen cash
for ink. Ho. Ho. Ho. Dear me. Fifteen
cash."

Kwan Tok felt his temper slipping. He
said, rather testily, "Twenty, then. Why do
you guffaw, honorable tradesman? Speak
the price. Days are coming and going—I
can't linger forever. If twenty won't do, do
tell me what will. I, myself, am a merchant,
and more than likely, will buy much goods
while in this country." At that the man of
the shop took on a calmer look, and replied,
"I ask permission to beg at least half a thousand pardons. Ten was so funny, and fifteen
so ridiculous that I forgot the courtesy due a
customer. My regular price is five cash, but
since you are a merchant, I charge three cash
only."

When Uncle Tok returned to the chamber
set apart for Ching and him, he received quite

a surprise. His package, instead of containing one ink cake, contained two. He said to Ching, "As I may have remarked, and as I am certain to remark again, this is a strange country. The merchant gave me two ink cakes for half the price of half a *one* and I, for one, am astonished." Kwan Ching thereupon voiced a thought of his own. "To my mind, the man who bought silk goods was even more remarkable. That person is a ting chay, he is if a tall hat means anything. Yet, he, a magistrate's runner, actually bought and paid for goods, instead of merely taking it. Nor did he strike the merchant. Having beheld such miracles I'm prepared for more. Probably the ghosts will not disturb—instead will soothe us."

But Kwan Tok removed all possibility of a ghostly visitation. With his cheaply bought ink he changed the door-sign to read "Ghosts please stay away," and under it, "Chieh is here." (Duke Chieh is the one greatly feared by all spirits.) That was enough, to be sure, but Kwan Tok, just to *be* sure, wrote further, "There's a rooster on my bed." And the

rooster, you know, is a thorough dispeller of
ghosts. He drives them away every morning.

With lantern and gong the watchman
walked. Bong. Bong. "One hour past hon-
est-men-in-bed." And later, Bong. Bong.
"Two hours past. Sleep sweetly." Bong.
Bong. Bong. "Thieves, I am watching you
closely." Lulled by the musical voice of him
who watched, Kwan Ching and Uncle Tok
soon went to sleep. Their weariness was
heavy upon them, they slept loudly. It required a dozen thumps upon the door to
break their slumber. Kwan Tok awoke first,
and called, "The ship is breaking up. All
hands to your swimming." Then his senses
returned to give full service, and he said
politely, "The house is secure, watchman.
Thank you for inquiring. Chin. Chin." An
outside voice protested. "Sir, I am not the
watchman. You have made an error rather
unflattering to me, though I can't think
you meant harm. I am the thief. THE
THIEF. Because of a lame foot, I sha'n't
be able to rob this house until late morning.
Kindly hide your money where it will be

pleasantly puzzling to find. And, by the way, you neglected to fasten your window."

Kwan Ching heard the thief's warning, and expressed his surprise. "Of all things ever, this is the oddest. Did he leave us a sword with which to fight him?" Uncle Tok said, "It is no more than I expected. I still contend that we are among remarkable men. I'll call the watchman." His shriek was answered before the echo passed. Over the sill vaulted a watchman. "Thieves warn, and watchmen come on call," murmured Kwan Tok. "But let me display no surprise. Thoroughly vigilant watchman, a thief will rob his house before morning." "I know. I know," repeated the watchman. "But don't be alarmed. He has orders to wear a dull sword. To cut throats is forbidden him." Such queer statements caused Kwan Ching to ask a question. "Honorable watchman, if your thieves are so given to obeying orders, pray tell me why you tolerate thieves at all? Why not order them to give up thievery?" The question was easy to answer. "If we did away with thieves, how would magistrates and watchmen gain a living? We hold our thieves quite necessary. They teach us precaution. Besides, they enable honest men to feel a great superiority."

Ching, too, could take precaution; as he proved by the thoroughness with which he secured the bolts.

When Uncle Tok and Kwan Ching again trod the streets, they kept their eyes alert for strange sights. Ching, with his gaze fixed upon a magnificent pagoda, bumped heavily into a passer by. Imediately sounded a crash, and the street ran yellow with broken eggs. "Run. Run," piped Ching. "Run, Uncle Tok, even as I do now. I've broken eggs." Ching, his queue askew and his feet lifting rapidly, dodged through the crowd. His great speed was enough to make the chase a long one. But it was not enough to gain him escape. When next he saw his uncle Tok, the two were in a magistrate's yamen. Uncle Tok used his finger to write in the air. "I'll take all the blame. If you are set free, be sure to hire many mourners." Kwan Ching nervously inquired, "Do you expect the

"Run, run," piped Ching. "Run, Uncle Tok, even as I do now."

sword?" His uncle wrote, "I'll be surprised if I'm not greatly surprised by the penalty. This is a remarkable country." Lictors clanged their gongs while the magistrate took seat. "Let the chief prisoner take his stand and offer defence."

Up rose Kwan Tok speaking, "Your Honor, I plead guilty. It is true I broke. . . ." A lictor shouted, "Witness, restrain yourself." And he thrust a silence-bit between Uncle Tok's teeth. The clerk's gong soon hushed a general laughter. An old greybeard now spoke. "Your Honor, the charges are true. While market going with my basket of eggs, I jostled a gentleman of foreign appearance. I dropped my eggs, and saw the street turn yellow. I plead to being an old man and out of my sense of precaution." The magistrate said, "The law states clearly that a man must not put all his eggs in one basket. Furthermore, you are too old and tremulous to carry eggs in public. Let the next prisoner plead." Kwan Ching thought that his time had come. He could think of no defence to offer, so he said, "I throw myself upon the court's mercy."

Whereupon a lictor threw him to the floor, and sat upon him, thus quickly ending his plea. A man of scholarly bearing stood forth. "I am an architect. My plans were followed in building the Eleven Story Pagoda. I admit full guilt." The magistrate frowned upon him. "The Eleven Story Pagoda was built in enormous proportions, and of such striking appearance that persons beholding it for the first time are wont to stare upwards for whole hours, thereby disrupting traffic, and leading to collisions. You deserve little mercy, I'm thinking. Next prisoner." His clerk explained that the street paver had fled the country, the basket maker was dead, various other accused persons were yet uncaught. The magistrate nodded. The clerk struck a gong.

Swept along by the crowd, Kwan Ching and his uncle presently found themselves in the street, free, and greatly rejoicing. On the way to their rooms they encountered a man who seemed as sad as they were jubilant. Kwan Ching placed a rich coin in the sad one's palm. He was not at all surprised when the sad person rejected his golden kind-

ness. "I don't need money," sobbed he of
the flowing eye. "Thank you, again and
again, but I can't accept gold for a grief no
gold can ease. I am past all aid, unless perchance some kindly man will take my place
in the chair." "This person may be the street
paver, or the basket weaver's spirit come in
day time," thought Ching. Therefore, he re-
frained from saying, "Gladly." Instead he
asked, "What is the nature of the aid desired? Besides my money, I have good aim
with an arrow." The man began to weep
afresh. "Your tongue is not black. You
couldn't aid, though willing."

Now, in the Lands of Sun Rise, a black
tongued man is a man respected. His tongue
is black, not because of untrue tales, but for
reason of his diligence. A scholar worth his
salt is ever thrusting the writing brush into
his mouth, to make it pointed, and so, improve his writing. The habit is quite necessary to success, because a scraggy brush forms
unsightly characters, and a slovenly written
paper is always rejected in the Hall of Examination.

Kwan Ching felt much depressed to think his learning had been so sadly undervalued. "My tongue is not black, that is truth, to be explained by saying I am on a travel. Sir, I hold a degree—Complete Scholar." "Then you are my brother-in-books, and I know will fail me not. This is the sadness that bows me down. Twenty years ago, I graduated to the ruffle of drums, and I rode the white horse to circle the town, so that all men might see me and offer respect." (Evidently he graduated First. Only a First may ride the Emperor's white horse.) "Since that triumphant hour I have studied constantly. I begin to hope that some day I shall gain a slight knowledge. But, alas, I have been appointed governor. Ignorant person that I am, I must rule a province. Will you not volunteer to serve in my stead?"

By great effort Kwan Ching made a reply. "Really, Honorable Governor, I can think of no suitable answer. I am dazed. Give me time to consider." Pondering deeply, he followed his uncle to the house.

A marine official came to the door. "My

department has secured another sailing vessel for your service. Our merchants have accepted your jute in exchange for an equal weight of silks. The cargo is safely in ship." When the marine official had retired from sight and hearing, Uncle Tok delivered an opinion. "This country, I continue to believe, is remarkable. Too much so. I fear it can't last very long. Tomorrow I point the ship for deep sea. Will you go, or will you be governor?" Ching replied, "I have long been wanting to be governor." And there the conversation stopped. Uncle Tok resigned himself to a lonesome voyage.

The ship put out in a spanking breeze. Cannon roared farewell in heavy charges. Uncle Tok, from the admiral's high window aft, waved parting salutes. He felt a trifle sad to be leaving Ching, but then, he thought, "Young men must have their ups in the world, and only the few can rise to governor height." He had done much talking to convince the now distant city of his appreciation. His throat had been made dry by words of warm esteem. Naturally, he soon took strides to the water cask.

Uncle Tok lifted the matting cover . . . and there sat Ching, rather ashamed, but perfectly cool. The merchant felt inclined to tease. "May I suffer a loss on my goods if I'm not in presence of the governor. Why are you here, in water, great man, instead of dry in a carven teakwood chair?" Kwan Ching whispered, "Ssshh. Don't talk so loud. I am here to hide. They tried to force me into taking office. . . . A governor has many responsibilities. Besides, I remember the graves and the cakes of home." And where he whispered, there he stayed, till the land astern dropped from the reach of eye.

There the story ends. Kwan Ching went home. What more need be said of him? His later marriage was unexciting. His appointment to a small magistracy held little of interest. His rise, years after, to the governorship of Kiang Sing is told in three short lines.

BITTER WATERS

A LITTLE girl came down from The Tiger's High Retreat. She was unutterably excited. "Daddy. Daddy. I saw. . . . I saw. . . ." "Now. Now," said the grey old person, her father. "Don't stammer. Wait until you have your breath." So, Mee Lee sat on a pilgrim stone for enough moments to be nearly a minute.

"I ran all the way from the cloud-edge to this turnip field where you are, Tieh Tieh (Daddy). I ran with speed, because of what

I saw. A great dust hides the King's road. For miles and more a dust springs up in the valley." Yang Tchong had lived long in the hills. He was not easily moved. Placidly he stated his opinion. "It's nothing of danger for us, Small One. Probably Oo Loong is crawling through the valley. The dragon —nothing more. Hungry—nothing less. Oo Loong's hunger makes empty houses."

Sometimes it happened Mee Lee was hard to convince. "But, a dragon doesn't crawl with colored flags. I saw reds and yellows beneath the dust." "It's only our friend Oo Loong. Oo Loong is a-foot in the valley." "A dragon never carries shining steel." "The steel belongs to those who dispute his right to dine. The low-land people scrimmage with scythes . . . but Oo Loong will have his dinner. I am glad our village holds a sworn agreement with the beast."

Yang Tchong never permitted himself to become excited. Therefore, when drummings and brassy noises came to his ears, he remarked them with a mere "Mmmmmm." And when he saw the roadway bright with spears, and high with bannerets, he still maintained an even voice. "Dear me. I think the whole world's army, and a few moon-men besides, are bringing weapons to our peaceful hills. King's Musketeers and Long Sword Men I think them, by their colors. Hearty eaters and clever thieves. Trouble. Trouble." He was not pleased. But Mee Lee's eyes sparkled, and by every little hop and skip, she was joyful, because of the music and the sight of pretty jackets.

"Yes, Master Captain," said old Yang Tchong. "These are the Pleasant Green Hills. At the turn of the road lies the Village of Ching Ling Tee. Behind, stands the Mountain called Huge Rocks Piled. Your guns are a useless burden, for you'll have no fight with us. We are good people—always in peace, Master Captain." The battle-chief eyed him with rancor. "Peaceful, perhaps, but stupidly reckless. I am General Huey, and my deeds of derring do are told of by every kiang kou jin (Tell-old-story-man) in the kingdom. Where can I find the dragon who has the name Oo Loong?"

"I am General Huey."

Old Yang Tchong again touched his forehead to the earth. "Please pardon me, Master General. Before this day a captain was the highest man I ever saw. We are orderly people here, Master General. We pay our taxes, and hope the King will live a thousand years. Have you brought a peace offering to the dragon?"

In Kiang Sing there's a monument to honor General Huey, but not one stone of it was placed in memory of his patience. A hasty, proud, three-feather wearer. "Lead on, old mountain fellow. Lead us to the dragon's cave. His Majesty, the Paramount King, sends us here to snip the dragon's horns. And that's a pleasant way to mean we'll kill him." Yang Tchong was still turtle-bobbing his head; hence he could smile in safety. "Oh. To kill the dragon. Then it's this way to go, Master General. There away, and up, and across, they say the dragon lives. We are timid people here, so we never visit the caves. Oo Loong eats whatever living thing may come to him. He is fierce, Master General, and hard to gin. The last army that came to take Oo Loong, went home in half, with no larger game than a rabbit." "Stop," snapped the general. "No. No. Not your toes, but your tongue. Lead on to the cave." He touched his sword point to Yang Tchong's very thin one jacket. And the guide led on, oh, *didn't* he.

The Mountain called Huge Rocks Piled was named by a teller of truth. It consists wholly of rocks and hard climbing. Every farther inch of it is higher, steeper, wilder. And Yang Tchong knew his mountain thoroughly, no matter what he had *said*. In consequence, the hours passed swifter than the miles. Soldiers stumbled and fell through their drums. Soldiers tripped and let off their guns. General Huey was valley born. Merely the exertion of holding to the saddle quite took his breath away. He spoke no threat, but his face most plainly exhibited his thoughts. Old Yang Tchong, valuing the life within him, knew he had rambled far enough. He turned aside, and with his tasting-finger pointed to an immense and almost suspiciously convenient cave.

"Have I not done well, Master General? In utmost promptitude I have led you— straight as a bow cord I have led you—to Oo Loong's den. Smell the sulphur. Behold the footprints. Oo Loong has a sulphury breath, and a heavy foot. And now, Master General, permit old Yang Tchong to hide." But General Huey was issuing the tablets of battle. Each wooden ticket bore a command. "Light the gun fires." "Drummers sound a rub-a-dub." "Make faces." "March."

The gunners touched fire to their pieces. The musicians, though nervous, went forward with screams on their lips and sticks to their drums. Into the cavern the army rushed, and the sulphury odor was unbearable, and men sickened and fell, and the day was terrible. Midst of the smoke and din, the soldiers blundered through the den, through the darkness of the mountain's core. At last, and they were thankful for it, they came to the other end. Once more they stood in sunshine and pure air.

The general asked them, "Did any of you take the dragon's horns?" Man and boy they answered, "No, our Great General. We didn't *see* the dragon. Hence, we couldn't snip his horns. But else than that, the battle was very successful."

That night the village elders met, in secret, to discuss grave problems. The mayor made a speech. "Some years ago this village made a bargain with the dragon. Oo Loong said to us, the elders, 'You protect me, and I'll protect you. When soldiers come to injure me, you villagers fight them in my defence. When a foreign dragon comes (large though he may be), I will fight him in your defence.' Thus said the dragon. And we broke saucers, and burned incense, and vowed to respect the agreement. Have we kept faith?"

Yang Tchong said, "As long ago arranged, I led the soldiers to a cavern never lived in by Oo Loong—miles from the dragon's lair. Oo Loong has no complaint of me. My duty was faithfully done." Another bearded one spoke. "As planned in the village council, I led our young men to the cave and hid them. When the soldiers came, we burned

sulphur, and threw huge stones on the low-
land rascals. Faithfully we did our duty,
fought in the dragon's behalf, as promised."

The mayor said, "Well done. Follow the
same plan tomorrow—if the army stays that
long. And now we have another duty. It
was further agreed that once each year we
should give to the dragon a girl or a boy.
Oo Loong takes hundreds from the valley.
We are supremely fortunate in losing only
one. The day of giving will shortly come.
Tonight we must draw lots. Let us decide
which child shall be given." Already the
scribe had written many names upon little
squares of paper, one name to each square. A
blind beggarman thrust his hand into a bowl.
After much nervous rustling he withdrew a
single name. The mayor whispered to the
scribe, and the scribe nodded. He knew his
own writing. "Mee Lee."

The others repeated, "Mee Lee. Mee Lee.
That is Yang Tchong's little girl, his little
girl. Yang Tchong is honored."

In the morning of the next day, Yang
Tchong said to his little daughter, "Mee Lee,

Small One, come with your poor old daddy
to the temple, for we must make offerings of
copper, and burn incense. Often you have
asked me whither went Yih Erh, your play-
mate, and always I have replied that only the
spirits could tell. But that was a deception,
child. Yih Erh was given, last year, to the
dragon. And now, oh, my beautiful daughter, be brave—for *I* am not. The lots have
been cast, and choice has fallen to you. Next
Sing Foon day our elder wise men will give
you over to Oo Loong. Alas. Alas. How it
is hard to give my little daughter to the
dragon."

Mee Lee was not at all tearful. Instead,
she seemed quite annoyed. "Why, honorable
Daddy, the wise men are silly. You know
very well that on the day Sing Foon I am
going down to my grandmother's, and she
will give me a doll—I think—she always
does. The village elders must choose another
day, because grandmother will be worried if
I fail to come. I shall talk to those wise
men." But Yang Tchong dispersuaded her.
"No. No. Little Daughter, that would bring

shame upon us. The village would not understand." He explained as best he could, using such terms as "Mistaken motive," and "True fortitude," and "Inescapable fate"— quite a jumble, and hard to understand. Thereupon, Mee Lee promised she'd say nothing to the elders. That was the only promise she made. And she kept it, too.

General Huey had taken a new guide each day. And each day had passed like the one before. The guide would say, "Oh yes, Master General. I know where the dragon lurks." And he would lead the army over precipice and roiling torrent, until the soldiers were ready to mutiny. And then he would point to a convenient cave and declare, "There the dragon lives. May I look upon his twisted horns when you have clipped them?" But the dragon was never found in the convenient cave. So General Huey became suspicious. He placed all the village elders under military arrest. He locked them in a dungeon, and promised them no good whatever. Furthermore, he set spies to watch upon the families of these unfortunate wise men.

The little girl, Mee Lee, went upon an errand, without really knowing where to go. She liked to walk the path named "Climbing to The Heavens." It passed through wilds of scented flowers, passed thrillingly close to musical waterfalls. So, that was the path selected. Mee Lee went much slower than her habit was. She carried a large basket and took precious care to keep it safe as she crossed the white-water streamlets and balanced on the cliffs. Close to a wide-fronted cavern, the little daughter of Yang Tchong began to call, "Oh, Master Dragon. Master Dragon-n-n-n? Are you within the hall? I have brought pleasant foods—fried young chicken, and jujubes, and melons, and cakes, and loquats, and a cup of sam shu—though it's cold. And now . . . may I visit my grandmother on the day of Sing Foon?"

Merely by chance she had come to Oo Loong's favorite haunt. Oo Loong rumbled in the lowest whisper he knew, "Go away. Get along. Go away on the back of a horse." (Meaning, "hastily.") Mee Lee obeyed him —took three steps. Then she called again.

"Master Dragon, do you mean . . ." "I mean if you don't go instantly, I shall blow devastating fire upon you." The surprised little visitor murmured, "Dear. Dear. Master Dragon is angry. But I shall leave my basket, and see what happens. If Oo Loong eats the fried young chicken, I simply *know* he'll give permission for the trip to grandmother's." She stirred the wine to raise its sweetness, and then went bounding down the path, glad that so much of her task lay behind.

Grim faces lifted from the boulders, and crafty eyes watched until Mee Lee passed beyond sight. Yellow fingers fluttered signals. They spelled success of the hunt.

The spies reported to General Huey. "We have found Oo Loong where he hides, in a cavern. There is no error in this finding. The dragon's voice was plainly heard. The glow of his breath was seen in cavern darkness. We followed a little village girl, and she led straight to the dragon's lair." General Huey commended them. "I am pleased with the success of your spying. Empty the powder catties into your guns. Sharpen spears. Tighten drum-heads . . . and think of your king as you fall."

Throughout that afternoon herds of frightened deer fled to the valley, and wild pigs hid in the water courses. The battle was terrific. Drums were beaten incessantly. Trumpets blared. The firelocks roared by squads and companies. But loudest of all was the dragon's scream, now in triumph, now in stark despair. General Huey ordered up all reserves, even those who guarded prisoners in the village. Then the screams of despair became more frequent. At length Oo Loong burst from his cavern. The exhausted soldiers could not restrain him. He spread his wings and was gone. The army followed him, not eagerly, but ordered, to have another fight.

They who dwelt in the Village of Ching Ling Tee came from hiding and danced in the streets. To the jow-wow-wowing of the distant going drums, they danced and gestured and shouted their happiness. The peace of olden times would now return. The hills were blue with smoke of incense.

Some days later the mayor said to his brother wise men assembled, "Oo Loong has sent a message. In it he accuses us of an unfaithful dealing. When he has slain the king and queen and leveled Chang An City, he will return to our village. He hopes, the message states, that we'll make tender eating. What shall we do? *Which* shall we do? Be eaten in peace? Or, give him a struggle?" One of the elders suggested, "We might abandon our glorious Village of Ching Ling Tee. We might scatter in as many directions as we are people. Surely then some few might escape." Yang Tchong said, "I have heard of a bookish magician living near the town Sim Tang. He is constantly making improved charms, said to be dragon-daunting. Let us send money to the magician, and put our trust in charms." The others said "Do." And the mayor added to their talk, "Capital. *You* go, Yang Tchong, and procure us infallible charms."

Even then, in the night time, Yang Tchong started on the perilous journey to get them charms. "Them charms" somehow sounds like very poor language, but there's no time now to change it.

The traveler inquired his way to the magician's dwelling, and he bought charm wares, and presently returned, without adventure or hindrance, to the village.

Every person, however large, no matter how small, in the village of Ching Ling Tee received a charm. The mayor jingled as he walked. Yang Tchong was often seen to smile. Howbeit, that is no reason for suspecting he had kept more than his share of charms. Perhaps he was merely remembering that the day of Sing Foon was past, and that his daughter had gone on a long-talked-of visit. She had gone to her grandmother's.

So Yang Tchong smiled. And smiling he remained . . . even when he beheld the dragon. Polite, too. "May you always have meat, Oo Loong." The distance between them was growing smaller. "May your wounds become whole." Yang Tchong was becoming more nervous than he liked to admit. "I wish you the five blessings. And now . . . I must go to the village."

Oo Loong plunged through the air.

That was a parlous moment. . . . Black art against a blacker dragon. Magic against muscle. A fierce desire for vengeance driving dusky wings so surely to the prey.

Yang Tchong wondered if he would experience pain. They say a dragon's bite is seldom felt. The creature's breath imparts a numbness to the flesh it strikes.

At arm-stretch distance the dragon fell. He had reached the circle of magic influence. No farther could he go. Charms had dispelled the lift from his wings. They enfeebled his legs. They stayed his forked tongue. He slumped in the dust. And Yang Tchong strolled leisurely to the village.

Day after day Oo Loong sought to take revenge upon the hill people. A charm always balked him. The villagers laughed; they struck him with clods, flicked him with switches to show their contempt. Once, while the dragon drank at a stream, little Mee Lee came with bucket and gourd. The child was unafraid. Her safety-charm was linked in a necklace. A very sympathetic person, she said to Oo Loong, "Please, Master Dragon, I am sorry they torment you so. If you'd really try to be nice, I'm almost sure you *could* be, and then all of us would like you."

Nothing could have driven Oo Loong to fiercer passion. The idea of a dragon's trying to be nice. He breathed flame and smoke till the rivulet seethed and seemed to burn.

Mee Lee sipped water from her gourd— and threw it down, much vexed. She reproached Oo Long, "You've ruined the spring, you ugly old dragon. Oh, yes, you have. How can you be so terrible? Now the people will beat you again. You'd better run, for I have heard them say they'll put a bridle on you and have you plow the fields." The dragon said nothing. He was trying to think. Few are they who can think and talk, all in a time together. When the ponderation had been successfully completed, Oo Loong lumbered off to a village well. He puffed his cheeks and blew a great sulphury breath upon

the water. From well to well, to stream, to pond, he visited every source of water. At last he had found revenge.

The village elders met to discuss a deep calamity. The mayor said, "We must die of thirst. Who can drink brimstone? Our wells are filled with bitter waters. No one can drink water containing Oo Loong's pestilential breath. The taste is unbearable. My throat is too dry to say more." Yang Tchong said, "When I once passed through the desert, where water is very bad, I boiled my drink in a pot with many onions. Immediately it became sweet. I lived, yes, I lived. The eye of the oldest among you can see that this is true." The mayor praised him, "Yang Tchong is a suggester of good plans. Let each man fill his kettle with sulphur water and onions. Then apply fire. Oo Loong is put to shame."

But the villagers foolishly taunted. Oo Long. "Thank you, dear Oo Loong, for breathing sulphur in the ponds. By so doing you compelled us to discover a wonder-

"You've ruined the spring, you ugly old dragon."

ful new drink. In the bitter waters we place —————— but there—we must not tell."

The dragon spied upon them and learned their secret. That night he visited every garden. He blew his flaming breath upon the onion plants and burnt them to their roots.

Next morning Yang Tchong said to his daughter, "Mee Lee, I have been hard at work, and have a parched throat. Fetch your weary old daddy a drink of onioned water." Mee Lee replied, "The dragon came in the night and puffed his breath on every onion. The patch is baked and bare." Yang Tchong exclaimed, "Why, the miserable rascal. But we'll outwit him. Boil me some tansy water." Mee Lee said, "Honorable Daddy, if I do, the dragon will come breathing live coals and blazes. That which happened to our onions will be happened to our tansy. But, I know a wild-growing plant that will give a nice taste to the water." She skipped down the hillside and gathered leaves from a shrub. In a very short while Yang Tchong satisfied his thirst. He said the taste was excellent; not a taint of sulphur remained.

When Oo Loong beheld the villagers gathering shrub leaves, he knew quite well their object. He began at once to breathe destructive fire. But Oo Loong was only a single dragon—he was not ten thousand. Having burnt all bushes from a little hill, he paused to rest and consider. Countless hills he saw, and every one of them green with shrubs. He couldn't destroy them in a double life-time. Useless to try. The weary dragon sighed, and stretched his wings.

Once more the mayor called his wise men to assembly. Said he, "Our village may now drink leaf water in security. Oo Loong has gone far to the west, vowing he'll never return. Our thanks are deserved by Yang Tchong. Let us give Yang Tchong's name to the leaves whose service he discovered." Yang Tchong said, "I am not worthy of the honor. Besides, my little daughter, Mee Lee, first used the leaves, and she is too modest for such fame. Let us give *everyone* honor for the discovery. Let us give our village name to the shrub of beneficial leaves . . . Ching Ling Tee, if it please you."

So that's the name today . . . Tee, or **Tea**, without the Ching, and dropping the Ling. Tea it is, and good it is. The drink of the village people is known where ever kettles steam.

* * * * *

I wrote this story exactly as the kiang kou jin told it in the market square. Somewhat pleased with it, I read it to Wu Chang, my gardener, and the gardener said, "That's merely the old Ning Poo story. No truth at all in it. A boy named Ah Tcha discovered tea." Wang Kwa, the cook, overheard. "How absurd," said Wang Kwa. "Everyone knows that tea was discovered by Sing Ah Sin."

That means I'll have to pay six cash for the story of "Sing Ah Sin and The Demon."

NOW IT IS WRITTEN

WANG WEE, on whom be peace, was no
worse for badness than the other dwellers in
Ping Shan Village. But . . . he climbed
the wrong sophora tree. And the Crow's reports were tinged with prejudice.

Wang Wee was landlord at the Inn of
The Three Little Soldiers. His roof was
tight in utmost of storm, the food he served
must be said rather good, and his beds were
very hard. The people of Kiang Sing have
an odd preference in beds. The harder they
are, the better they sleep, and the more the

landlord charges. But the travelers who stopped at Wang Wee's inn were poor men, down to a man. They ate but sparingly, and stayed not long.

It's changeable weather in Kiang Sing when the spring begins to break. It rains all day in Kiang Sing, but changes at night— and simply *pours*. A richly dressed mandarin, military class, entered the inn, and said to the beaming landlord, "Plague take such days as the Rain Shen gives us. This is the worst weather that ever came over the hill. The roof of my sedan chair is a letter-in of rain. A bed, a candle, a pipe . . . good stories and hot, nice foods—have you these things? If so, I'll end my travel for the day, and be a fourth warrior at the Inn of The Three Little Soldiers." Travelers, it seems, must ever have their little witticisms.

Wang Wee laughed appreciatively. "Ho. Ho. Ho. As for the Three Little Soldiers (that was merely the name of the Inn), I'll throw them out, and a few donkey drivers with them. There'll be no lack of room. Oh yes, Honorable Military Mandarin, I can give you the best accommodation. Has Your Generalship traveled far? What is your sing that will please me so? What is the sound of your ming? Tell me your beautiful tsze."

The traveler replied, "Han is my family name. The ming is Ching. My added flowery name is Chu. I hold a commission in the Extraordinary Tiger Troops, and am very wealthy. Yes, excessively wealthy—and only a few years ago I was poorer than a beggar's hated step-child."

A host should always be polite. Wang Wee asked further questions. "Is that true? How *much?* Well. Well. I offer congratulations. Tell me, Militarily Great Han Ching Chu, how you acquired in such short while your wealth that amazes poor Wang Wee." "Gladly," said the rich one. "A whim of fashion wealthied me. The ladies of the Queen's court fancied a new cosmetic for their hair. The chief ingredient of that cosmetic is—pheasant egg. With other soldiers I was sent to Hu Pei forest, there to guard the egg gatherers. I had sharp eyes, and found many nests. Now, my camels cover acres, and my house is the finest in Chang An City."

"Remarkable," exclaimed the landlord. "Exceptional, but perfectly true. Tell me, Great General, do the Chang An maids still gloss their hair with pheasant egg cosmetic?" "More than ever before. Better still, the men have taken to it. And the prices paid are higher." General Han Ching Chu named a sum of money that widened Wang Wee's eyes.

"By the best red idol in the temple, he tells a remarkable yarn." Wang Wee dropped too much pepper in the lotus nut soup. He was thinking of pheasant eggs. Wang Wee placed fire-wood in the rice pot. He had intended to fill the stove—but his thoughts were centered on pheasant eggs. Pheasant eggs. Pheasant eggs. The keeper of the inn could think of nought but pheasant eggs. "If I," he said to himself, "could only find some pheasant eggs, some pheasant eggs, why, I'd make more money on one little nest of pheasant eggs than ever I've made in a year of tending inn. I wish the day would pretty up.

I'd go to the woods and hunt for pheasant eggs. I would. I'd do what I say—hunt for the eggs of the pheasant."

A wind came up and herded the clouds out to sea. Kiang Sing was beautiful, under springtime skies. The desirous inn-keeper bought a wicker three bushel basket and kept the promise he had made to himself. He wandered through the woodland, seeking pheasant eggs. But fortune wasn't with him. He couldn't seem to find the nests, or else they belonged to the year before, and held nothing but broken shells. Time after time Wang Wee peered down in his basket and murmured, "Oh, dear me. Not a single egg is in the basket. I haven't found an egg. But persistence wins in the end. Walk another li, walk another tash, I'll yet find the nest of a pheasant." He glanced at a sophora tree, and there—he saw a nest.

The little keeper of the inn stood on his basket and made an upward leap. He grasped a limb and soon was high in the tree. But the nest—what a pity—was very far out, on a limb-tip. And Wang Wee—how de-

plorable, just then—had always eaten well.
He was fat. And because of his fatness—
heavy. The limb bent more, and Wang
crawled farther, and then there came a horrid, breaking sound.

And a farmer was saying, aggrievedly,
"Really this savors of unkindness, Honorable
Wang Wee. You deliberately climbed the
highest tree you could find, and from it leapt
into my dolicho patch." Wang Wee quickly
denied this accusation. "Nothing of the kind,
Most Handsome Farmer. Being in your vegetable patch is not at all what I intended. I
climbed the tree to get the eggs of a pheasant."

Then that unkind farmer laughed madly.
"Ho. Ho. Ho. He climbed a tree to gather
pheasant eggs. May I lose my queue if this
isn't funny. Why, Honorable Keeper of The
Inn, the nest belonged to a crow. It is true.
I'll show you its proof, on the wing." A crow
flew in circles above them. "Caw. Caw.
Caw." His brother crows and his cousins
came to aid him in the scolding. "Caw. Caw.

Caw." Their din was frightful. They dived, as if to attack.

Seven sticks, six straws, five strings, and

Then that unkind farmer laughed madly

several feathers—I'll give you my word that was all of the nest. But one might have thought it a mansion, to hear the crow as he grieved. Wang Wee hurled a clod. Then he went home, in a limp. His wicker three bushel basket contained exactly no eggs of the pheasant—and not one egg more.

It is doubtful if the inn-keeper gave a slightest further thought to the crow. But the crow was frequently near. Throughout the summer, often he circled the inn. Then, one morning, the roof tiles sparkled, and foolish persons said, "Just as I prognosticated, we had a frost last night. Autumn is come. I hear the wild geese crying south. There goes a robin. South. Going south." But the Wise Men said, "There's no more song in the liliac tree. Our many birds of the summer have flown to Spirit Land. They have gone to tell Great Yama how this man sinned, and that man aided a neighbor. The birds have gone to file their yearly reports with Yama."

An old black Crow strutted importantly into Yama's vasty, high-arched hall. "A bad report is all I bring, Great Yama. They on the earth were terrible, this season past. Wang Wee, of the Inn of The Three Little Soldiers,

Ping Shan Village, is the man under my jurisdiction. If you have words meaning worse than bad, then those are the words to use. Dip your pen, Great Yama. Write of the man Wang Wee. . . . He destroyed my nest, and broke all *thirty* eggs. He turned poor donkey drivers out in the storm, and thereby made room for mandarins. He charged three cash for a bowl of rice. He burned the cheapest incense he could buy. He pulled up radishes without first bowing to the Earth Spirits. . . ." Yama had been eating dates and figs; listening with only mild interest. Now he used both hands on his book, turning pages. His brow was crinkled. "Again, Crow, the name. Repeat the name. Wang . . . Wang . . ."

"Wee. Wee. Wang Wee, Great Yama. Wang Wee. The worst scamp in Ping Shan Village." Yama frowned. "Wang Wee??? Why do you come with nonsense, Crow? The name isn't written. There's no such person as Wang Wee in all the world. You, of course, spent the summer in idleness. And at the last moment hatched a name with which to deceive me. Go, Crow. Attend to your duties—and give up false-telling. Deception wakes my anger." And this, mark you, was said in no ordinary voice.

There was nothing of a prideful strut in the Crow's hasty leaving. The midnight-colored rascal went forth in terror. He was thoroughly puzzled. What could Yama mean —"There is no such person"? No *Wang Wee?* The Crow talked to himself. "Maybe I didn't pronounce the name in the way Great Yama sounds it. That must be the reason. I'll be more careful next time. Goodness me, my heart is pounding. Oh, yes, I'll be quite careful another time."

Back on earth in early spring, the Crow kept closest watch on the man Wang Wee. Whenever Wang Wee had a quarrel with the neighbors, the Crow was sure to be in some not far paulownia, or in an oil-tree, listening and remembering. "Bad words he used, and I think he tried to twitch his neighbor's queue. I shall speak of this to Yama. Caw. Caw. Caw." The black watcher grew in boldness with the summer. Frequently he

Yama murmured the name. "Wang Wee. Wang Wee."

perched on the roof-ridge. Sometimes he slept there, hoping to hear Wang Wee speak evil in a dream. His hatred actually increased. Merely because Wang Wee, unintentionally, had destroyed a half-built nest.

The time of chrysanthemum blossoms came, and all the birds took flight. Black Crow paraded into Yama's record hall. "This is my report, Great Yama, sworn to be correct. The man's name is Wang Wee. . . . *Wang Wee* . . . and that's the best I can pronounce it. Wang Wee is an unqualified knave. All villainies are his . . ."

Yama murmured the name. "Wang Wee. Wang Wee." His thumb riffled the pages. "Mmmmmmm. . . . Aren't you the same Crow that came last year with a false report? I thought so. Now hear what I say, Crow, and be guided. No man in the world today is named Wang Wee. I wish to hear no more of him. Don't come again to tell me the imaginary badnesses of a wholly mythic man. If you *do*—I'll put two hands to your neck, Crow, and give a crunching twist, Crow, and never more you'll see the fields take color in the springtime, *truthless Crow.*"

Safe away from Yama's hall, the old Crow talked to himself. "Whewwwh. An army could march to the noisy drumming of my heart. What a fright Great Yama gave me. Upon my word, I'll never go back again. *No,* not I. Let Wang Wee villain himself as he pleases. Crow will close his eyes to all misdoings."

Next year, and for many years succeeding, a moody old Crow wintered in the bright Moluccas, very, very far from Yama's hall. The Crow kept his word. He never again reported sins and deeds of kindness.

Wang Wee's queue turned grey. The carpenter said, "Will you buy a nice coffin? Eighty years old is like a candle in the wind. Ninety is like frost on the pantiles. You, Wang Wee, are ten years past the frost-age." Wang Wee answered, "The years go light with me. Sell your coffins to the young men. I shall step over the charcoal pan in my fifth happy marriage this evening."

The years went on into centuries. And
Wang Wee lived, and lived. The people
said he was three hundred. Lived and lived.
Of course he had his troubles, for life isn't
all honey and smile every day. Occasionally
he was sad—when he thought of his wives.
Not that they had mistreated him—not that.
But because he couldn't remember them all.
To save him, he couldn't remember how many
times he had wived. Thirty, or forty, he
wasn't sure. And Wang Wee lived, and
lived. The people declared his age was not
a minute less than four hundred years, and
a year.

King Chieh Chung was very fond of history. He kept several ancient story-tellers in
the palace, to recite their legends of the flowery past. Often the old men squabbled. One
of them would say an event happened thus
and so; whereupon another would declare,
"Not true. It happened in the way I told it
Tuesday night." The king complained to his
chancellor, "These story-tellers—who can believe them? They didn't see the battles of
which they prate so glibly. They have their

stories from other men, who got *their* stories from other men, and they, from others. I'd like to hear the truth. Isn't there any extremely old man who saw the Battle of Chee Hing Soo?"

The chancellor arched his brows. "Oh, Your *Majesty*. That was *three hundred* years ago. But I have heard of an unbelievably ancient man, in Ping Shan Village." He turned and spoke to a messenger. "Run to Ping Shan Village. Tell Wang Wee, the inn-keeper, he is wanted at the palace."

The king palmed his chin as if to think. "Chancellor, why can't we have a way to transmit messages other than by word of mouth? That messenger will forget every word, before he has run a dozen days. He is an awfully stupid fellow—hasn't half the head of yonder impish parrot." The parrot awoke. "Hello, King. Give Polly half of your spice cake." The chancellor replied—to the king, "La. La. Your Majesty. This long time past, our best minds have been trying to invent a better message sending system. If only we could strike upon a method to put the words on a paper, that would be grand. We have already decided on a name for it, when, as, and if, invented. It will be called 'Writing.' But I doubt if we'll ever see it."

Wang Wee was so old and frail that the king wouldn't let him kou tou (bump head). "My word," said the king. "He *does* look old. What is your age, grizzled inn-man?" "Dear only knows, Your Majesty, Sir. I stopped counting birthdays some two hundred years ago." The king glanced at his chancellor with the slightest closure of an eye; called, I believe, a wink. "No doubt, aged person, you served your country valiantly in the famous battle of Chee Hing Soo." Wang Wee shook his head. "Alas, no, Your Majesty. I was then too *old* to fight. But I saw the battle from a hillock, and can describe it well. Our army was led by Your Majesty's Great-great-great-great-great-great-grandfather. He was a fine king, Majesty, but not the equal of your Great-great-and-great-eight-times-again-grandfather. Han Ching Chu—I saw him long before he took the throne. He stopped at my inn, and talked pleasantly enough. As a very poor soldier he gathered pheasant eggs, and prospered to be king."

A parrot sauntered into Yama's vasty, high-arched hall. This parrot was a flagrantly over-bold fellow. "Greetings to you, Great Yama. I have come to report. The king hasn't done much mischief. He pulled out one of my feathers. That's the extent of his evil. Neither was the chancellor very bad. He threw a cup of wine at me. But then, I had called him laughable names. . . . There's a new man under my jurisdiction. The name is Wang Wee. Wang Wee is a nice old chap. Write good words for him, Great Yama." Yama's thumb had turned the pages. He narrowed his eyes to gaze at the parrot. "Wang Wee. Wang Wee. I have heard that name before. But it isn't in the book."

"Oh, yes, Yama, it must be. Old Wang Wee, of Ping Shan Village."

Yama's chin was thrust well forward. "The name isn't here, I tell you. There is no such man as Wang Wee."

That parrot was even more impudent than

I thought him. He screeched, "But I know very well there *is*. I see him every day."

Great Yama's hand came down on the book. The table crashed to the floor. Is it necessary to say that Yama was furious? Mmmmmm. His eyes held ill for a certain parrot. But the parrot was perched on a highest arch.

* * * * * *

Yama took up his book. And, "Come down, Parrot." he said. "It's my mistake. The pages were stuck together. I am very fond of dates and figs, and that accounts for Wang Wee's sheet being stuck to a page long finished. If I hadn't thumped the book so hard, I might have let Wang Wee live a thousand years." Yama tore out the page. It was rather sticky and far from neat. On a new, clean leaf he copied the record of old Wang Wee, speaking each word as he wrote it. "Wang Wee, to be born in the tavern of Three Little Soldiers, Ping Shan Village, in the year of the sheep. First report: He cries entirely too much. Struck nurse with a willow wood spoon. Second report: Unkind to the very nice wonk (dog). Threw the papa-man's boots in the stove. Broke nurse's yellow gemmed comb."

With great similitude the entries were continued to "Twenty-eighth report." A long blank space followed. And at the bottom was written, "One week after the seventy-third report, Wang Wee will fall in Ho Lan River. His grave will be on the Hill of Soughing Pines."

Yama dropped the pen. "Now it is written." And he chuckled. "Goodness me. That old person has already lived five hundred years. And *I* can't have him till *forty-five* more reports have been made. I hope he'll live wisely hereafter." Yama crumpled the sticky, ancient record and tossed it in a corner. And there the parrot found it.

King Chieh Chung entered his study one evening before the candles had been given a flame. He tripped on a chair, and went down —CRASH. The parrot awoke and began to scream, "*Pardon me, Great Yama. Pardon me. Oh, pardon me.*" Servants hastened in with light. His Majesty, having scolded the fellows, took a ball of crumpled paper from the floor. The paper was partly covered with strange black marks. "Mmmmmmm," said the king. "What's this? It's something upon paper, but very mysterious to me." And all the while the parrot screeched, "Pardon me, Great Yama. Pardon me."

Now King Chieh Chung was a man of perspicacity. He listened to the parrot's excited appeal, and said, "*Yama*. Yama is the word, no doubt of it. That crazy parrot has been to Yama's Land to make reports; and I dare say received a thorough fright. I wonder if he brought this paper from Yama's Land. If so, these marks are written words, for we know that Yama puts his reports on paper."

Long sat His Majesty, staring, pondering. He placed a finger on one of the marks, and promptly the parrot clamored, "Wang. Wang. Wang." The royal golden finger was placed on another mark. "Wee. Wee. Wee," shrieked the parrot. The royal finger moved again, and moved again. The parrot chanted, "San. San. San." (Three. Three. Three.) "Mmmmmmm," said the king.

"Three little marks. Why, that must surely be Yama's way of writing 'san' on paper."

The parrot was in his noisiest humor. "Yin. Yin. Yin." "I'll vow," declared the king, "this scratch mark *looks* like a man. And what could this other mark be but 'shan'? (mountain). It looks like a shan. . . . Chancellor. Oh, Chancellor . . . Chancellor, come."

Three of them worked day and night. King, chancellor, and parrot, they deciphered Yama's page. At the end of a week King Chieh Chung could write a hundred different words. It was easy enough to invent a few more characters. His Majesty taught the queen and the cook to write. They were all in the palace together, but he made them write him letters every day. He taught his many Wise Men—and, of course, that ends the story. Now it is written. Chah bah doah.